MARIA RIVERA

Chasing The Wind

Editor - Denise Harmon

Book Cover Designer - Amanda Wilmot

Scriptures from the Bible taken from the New Living Translation

First edition

ISBN: 978-0-578-91522-7

Advisor: Amanda Wilmot

*This book was professionally typeset on Reedsy.
Find out more at reedsy.com*

This book is dedicated to Jesus Christ, my Lord and Savior and to my daughter, Amanda Wilmot.

"I observed everything going on under the sun, and really, it is all meaningless-like chasing the wind."

Contents

Acknowledgement

I would like to start by thanking Jesus Christ, my Lord and Savior for giving me the privilege to write this story and showing favor at every corner.

* * *

My precious daughter, Amanda Wilmot, thank you for encouraging me to start writing again. Thank you for continuously telling me to trust myself as a writer and for reading countless chapters in a timely way and providing feedback. You are the best writer I know. My sweet girl. My rock. My friend.

* * *

My sister-in-law Jessica Ferrer, daughter in-law, Roshni Gunness Fernandez, and friend, Joy Hickock – My first three readers from beginning to end. Your encouragement and support has meant the world to me.

* * *

My sons, Michael and Eric, thank you for your encouragement and support.

* * *

My husband, Paul, thank you for doing location research with me and honoring when I needed hours and hours to write.

* * *

My son-in-law Adam, and dear friend Maggie Oquendo, thank you for technological guidance.

* * *

My grandon AJ for keeping a smile on my face.

* * *

Mom and Dad, thank you for keeping my Spanish intact!

* * *

Kathy Carbone, thank you for listening always and clarifying scripture for me.

* * *

Pastor Jim Detweiler, thank you for your amazing preaching

that basically became the short sermons in this book.

* * *

Pastor Lou Zinnanti, thank you for allowing me to serve in Honduras.

* * *

John and Maritza Hernandez, my Cuban friends and role models.

* * *

Pastor Melvin Flores, an inspiration for many.

* * *

The people of Honduras, you remind many of what's important.

* * *

Washinton Heights, you will always be my neighborhood.

* * *

Finally, friends and family. Read carefully and find yourselves. There's a little bit of you in every one of these characters.

Chapter 1

◦◦◦◦◦

August 2015

Washington Heights, New York

Manhattan is known as a beautiful, glamorous city. Times Square, the Theater District, Little Italy, and the artsy, eclectic villages are magnets for tourists and dreamers seeking a career. About fifteen miles north of Midtown, buried in the borough of Manhattan, is Washington Heights. A part of the city that tourists rarely visit. However, those who live there believe it is the safest place in New York and definitely the friendliest. People help each other. Take care of each other. Protect each other. That's important because it's where twenty-one-year-old Marisol Colucci lives.

She stands 5'3", with hazel eyes that compliment her curly, chestnut brown, shoulder-length hair. A warm undertone complexion sprinkled with light freckles makes her appear like a schoolgirl. No one could ever guess the nightmare she had been through when she arrived in the city on May 29th. And it had been one month since she had received an envelope with no return address that simply bought her time.

Each floor of the building in which she lives has four apartments, and 2C, which is Marisol's, is in a corner nestled against 2B as if it were seeking protection. Immediately to the right of the front door is a spare room that Marisol uses to make wine. A long hallway is punctuated with a small bathroom on the right, and then a few steps farther bring you to the kitchen, also on the right. Five steps farther down the hallway is a single-paned French door that leads to the living room, and on the opposite side of the living room, two French doors open to a large master bedroom with a smaller bedroom to the left. A window in the master bedroom is for the fire escape, which serves as a makeshift terrace. In the brief time she has lived there, she has made it home with personal touches. Although she did not have a work permit, she secured employment at La Esquinita Discount store, which is a two-minute walk from the apartment.

Summers in New York are brutal, and this one was no different. Each day after work, she relaxed on the fire escape with her Bible and a glass of wine. She was immersed in scripture until she heard a male voice escalating from 2B.

"I broke it off because I wasn't sure."

Marisol looked to her left and noticed that her new neighbor's window was open.

"It doesn't matter how much her parents had already spent. I wasn't going to marry someone I was not in love with." The frustration in Felipe's voice grew as he continued to unpack boxes. "Listen...no....just listen. We'd slowly drifted apart and a lot of it was because she assumed I would want to open an office in some upscale neighborhood in Connecticut."

There was a silent pause.

Chapter 1

De Madre. He must be getting an earful from whoever he is talking to, Marisol thought as she got closer to his window, struggling to stay out of sight.

"This has absolutely nothing to do with being a good Christian, Mom. Come on! You know what? I'm done. No, we'll—"

Suspecting he was about to hang up, she scurried back to her side and sat.

"Sure. Sure. Okay, goodbye." He threw his cell phone, and it landed under the window that led to the fire escape.

He went to retrieve it and noticed the beautiful brunette sitting outside.

"Hey, I'm sorry you had to hear that," he said as he stepped out to get fresh air.

Felipe Ortega stands at six feet. He has short jet-black hair combed back with deep brown eyes to match. The twenty-seven-year-old doctor was doing his residency at New York—Presbyterian Hospital, which is a short distance from the apartment he had recently rented.

"Hear what?" she smiled. "I'm Marisol."

"I'm Felipe. I see you sitting out here often and have thought about introducing myself, but I didn't want you to think I was some weirdo."

"Who says I don't already?" she replied as she stood and warmly shook his hand.

"Oh, wow. Shot down twice today. Okay." He smiled, and that's when she noticed he had killer dimples.

She smiled shyly and sat down.

"You work at La Esquinita Discount store, right?" he asked.

"Yes. You have come in a few times and you looked a little familiar, but I couldn't place you. I'm there Monday through

Friday and some Saturdays. I work the day shift, thank God."

"Yeah, thank God," he said with a mocking tone.

"You sounded a little sarcastic when you said that."

"I didn't mean to. I just have a lot going on now. Listen, I've enjoyed talking to you, but I've got to get ready for work now."

"What do you do?"

"I'm a doctor," he replied, wanting to chase the words back into his mouth.

Marisol's eyes bugged out of her face and she could not suppress the smile.

"Listen, I love my neighborhood, but I have to ask because you are probably the only doctor in this building and possibly the entire block. Why don't you live in, you know—mmm?"

"A more affluent neighborhood?" he asked. She nodded.

"Long story. But I'm off tomorrow. Meet out here?"

"Sure. Around five-thirty?"

"That sounds good. Unless, of course, your husband or boyfriend will have an issue with it," he added for good measure.

"I don't live with anyone. Long story," she replied.

"All right, then five thirty it is," he flashed her another smile "Listen, I don't know anyone in this building and it's always good to have a neighbor's number. So take my number and then text me yours."

"Okay," Marisol agreed.

* * *

"Push, Mrs. Alvarez, push. Almost. You can do this!" Esperanza Alvarez sat up with the help of her husband, and turning redder than a tomato gave one final, sweaty push after

4

which she heard Dr. Ortega yell, "It's a girl!" He watched as the couple bonded with their baby. It was one of the most satisfying moments of being an ob-gyn, and it was the type of work that kept Felipe hopeful about his life.

After a long night, Felipe relaxed in the cafeteria with a cup of coffee and a magazine.

"Is this seat taken, sir?" Bernie asked.

Bernardo Gonzalez, a fifty-year-old man who has lived and worked in Washington Heights for the past fifteen years is an ER doctor. Not a tall man, but distinguished-looking, he wears his short gray hair neatly combed back. He has kind, soulful brown eyes, a gentle demeanor, and an accent that gives him a sophisticated distinction. Having emigrated from Cuba with his wife Rosa and their then five-year-old daughter Fatima in the late 90s, he had re-validated his medical degree in America.

"Hey, Bernardo! It's been too long." Felipe stood hugged him and then made room for the man who had been his mentor when he first arrived at New York-Presbyterian Hospital. "Are you still working in the ER?"

"I am," Bernie, as he was affectionately called by friends, responded as he bit into his sandwich.

"Wow. How was it tonight?" Felipe asked.

"Your usual shootings, MVAs, a little kid that swallowed a quarter, and one dude that shot his wife with a shotgun at close range. That was pretty much the first hour."

"Sounds stressful."

"It can be. What about you? How are things in the maternity unit?"

"I delivered four babies and just left three women in phase 1 of labor." He rubbed his eyes from exhaustion.

"Still commuting from Connecticut?"

"No. That got old quickly, and things got tense at home after I broke up with Sandra. So I rented an apartment about seven minutes from here."

"Your mom still giving you grief about that?"

"Yep. She thinks I made a big mistake and that I could have had a—let's see…" He paused like one does when wanting to quote someone precisely. "A lucrative future with Sandra. You know, two doctors are a dynamic combination in my mother's estimation. I'm over it. She needs to get over it too."

"How's your brother?"

"Alex is great. He's also working in the city and getting fed up with the commute as well, so I'm guessing he'll be moving soon too."

"Is he still practicing immigration law?" Bernie asked casually.

"Yeah. Why?"

"Just wondered."

"Oh. Hey, how are Rosa and Fatima? I see them occasionally when I stop at the discount store."

"They're good. Fatima's in her final year at John Jay College and is talking some nonsense about joining the NYPD as soon as she graduates."

Felipe laughed. "Hey, speaking of the pharmacy. There's a girl that works there that I just found out is my neighbor."

"Marisol?" Bernie asked. "Dark brown curly hair, has a few freckles?"

"Yeah, that's her. Did Rosa just hire her?"

Bernie measured his words carefully. "You could say that. She has become like a daughter to us. You know we live in the building across the street from Marisol, and well, now you.

She got here in May, and she's been through a lot." He paused reflecting on it. "So now that you're living in the city, you have no excuse not to say yes."

"Say yes to what?" Felipe played dumb.

"You know what I'm talking about. When are you going to visit my church?"

"When you stop asking," he whispered into Bernie's ear as he patted him on the back before he left.

"Get some sleep," Bernie responded as Felipe waved good-bye.

* * *

The August oppressive heat never agreed with Marisol, but she made the best of it by sitting on the fire escape during the late afternoon hours. She enjoyed a glass of wine while she meditated on God's word and talked to Him about her day. *Heavenly Father, thank you for keeping me safe today. Thank you for the opportunity to work and earn a living.* She was in the middle of her early evening winding down when she heard the window next to hers open.

"Hey, there he is." She smiled at Felipe who was struggling with his glass of wine.

"Am I interrupting? You looked lost in thought," he replied as he made himself comfortable.

"No, I was just sharing my day with God."

Her honesty caught him off guard.

She broke the awkward silence. "So how was your day?"

"Actually, I just woke up."

"Must be nice!"

"I ended up staying overnight at the hospital because they

were short-staffed."

"Oh, that's right, you're a doctor. Emergency room, right?"

"No."

"Pediatrics?"

"No, I'm an ob-gyn." She shifted her position and he noticed that she was turning red. "Are you blushing?" he asked Marisol with a half-smile.

She put her hands on her face. She stood up and started fanning herself with her hands as she twitched her nose like she did when she was fibbing or flustered. "No, it's the heat and my cheeks get red when it's hot," she bluffed. She cleared her throat and changed the subject. "So what's your story? I mean, the other day on the phone you sounded really mad. You said it was a long story." She sat, picked up her wine, and said, "You know, they say that confiding in strangers sometimes is good because there is objectivity."

He smiled at her philosophical bait.

"So I'm all ears," she said as she sat and made herself as comfortable as you could get on the fire escape.

He sighed. "My ex-fiancé and I had been together since our first year of college. We both attended Yale medical school, and in our senior year, we got engaged. We had put off setting a date because we weren't sure where we would complete our residencies, and that's where the problems began."

"Does she have the same specialty?"

"No, she is an oncologist. So when it came time to apply for residency programs, I applied for Presbyterian Hospital here in the city and she went out of her mind. We had several, I mean multiple, conversations about what our future would look like now that the future was looking like the here and now, and it seemed to me like she had forgotten why she had become a doctor. All she talked about was starting a practice in a cash-rich part of Connecticut, and I wanted to come to the city. She started changing, and I realized it was all about money for her. And there were a lot of other things. Marrying her would have been unfair to us both. You know what I mean?" He looked over and noticed that she was nodding sympathetically.

"How did you break up with her?" Marisol asked.

"Well, that's where I become a jerk," Felipe sheepishly admitted as he shifted positions. "I broke up with her two days before the wedding." He looked at her to observe her reaction.

"It must have been a tough decision, and it couldn't have been easy for either of you."

"It's funny that you say that. The night I broke it off, the first thing she said was 'after all the money my parents spent' which honestly indicated to me she was just thinking of material things. She would have married me even if she knew I was not happy." He paused a few seconds and then said, "I don't even think she loved me. It was the idea of me. Of being married to a doctor or someone equal to her station in life. Something ridiculous like that."

"Did your family support you?" she asked, guessing what the answer would be.

"My brother and father, yes. My mother is disgusted with me. She feels I was being selfish and not considering Sandra or her family's feelings. I admit, when I was in high school and in my early years of college I dated around and was a bit of an idiot."

"You? Nah," Marisol teased.

"No, seriously. I was selfish in high school and not much

better the first two years of college, but I changed," he paused. "This decision was a responsible one. And then, of course, there's the church's opinion."

"Why would the church have anything to say?"

"Where I come from? Why wouldn't they?"

"Did you attend church together?"

"We did. And everything was fine until I broke up with her and I stopped going."

"Why?"

"Because even though I went to a different service to avoid her, I got tired of people whispering behind my back and giving me the cold shoulder."

"How was that God's fault?"

"Oh, you sound like Bernie," he mumbled.

"Gonzalez? Oh, that's right, he's a doctor at Presbyterian. His wife Rosa and I have been friends for a couple of months. She's also my boss. You know they live in the building across the street."

"Yeah, he told me last night. He was my mentor when I started working at the hospital and was good to me. I know Rosa and Fatima too. Fatima's a little crazy, but she's all right. Nice family. I told him you were my neighbor."

"Well, it took courage to do what you did in breaking off your engagement."

"Thank you. That's what my dad and brother think."

"What's your brother's name?"

"Alex."

"Younger or older?"

"Younger. Why twenty questions?" he smiled as he asked.

"It's important! It gives me a complete composite of you. Remember what I said. Since I don't know you, your family, or Sandra, it's an objective analysis."

He smiled and said, "So you don't think I'm a jerk?"

"No, not at all. Besides that, I'm not in the business of judging people." She smiled at him warmly and he reciprocated.

"Well, you said your story is complicated too. So let's have it," he said.

"It's complicated all right. Okay, from the top."

"Wait! Another glass of wine? I'll provide this time and you can next time."

"Sure." She waited while he refilled their glasses and carefully thought out how she would explain her story. What could she be forthcoming about? Her story was just a braid of staggering complications. Should she tell him everything? *Heavenly Father, please guide my words. I don't have many friends and I feel you've sent me a good one. Please guide my words and...*

"You're lost again in your own world," he said, offering her glass back to her. She stood, and that's when he noted her petiteness and the light freckles on her cheeks.

"No, I was just thinking about how late it is. How I ended up here is not quite so simple and I have to start like way back."

He made himself even more comfortable. "I'm ready. You're not getting out of this. What's fair is fair. I spilled my guts. Your turn," he responded.

Chapter 2

"**M**y parents were missionaries in Honduras. My dad, Vincent Colucci, was born and raised in Italy. He came to the United States and attended Liberty University in Virginia and earned a bachelor's degree in Biblical Studies. He went back to his church in Italy and worked there as an associate pastor. He had a strong desire to start a center for victims of human trafficking, specifically women and children. The center was like a shelter for them where they received an education, job counseling, and of course, the word of God. My dad had been on a couple of mission trips to Honduras with his church in Italy, so it's where he wanted to do this. He connected with a church there and opened up the center."

Felipe was completely engrossed in her story when he asked, "How did he meet your mom?"

"She was a teacher in Tegucigalpa and applied to teach at the center. They married about two years after they met. Her name was Esperanza."

"Wow. It's interesting that your father is Italian and your mom is Hispanic."

"Yeah, hey, we never got into your heritage."

"Father Cuban. Mother Italian. Carry on, Colucci. You keep referring to your parents in the past tense. Why?"

"I'm getting to that. El Nuevo Día, or New Day, was the name of the center. It had been up and running for twenty-five years and was going well. Women and children were getting the help they needed in becoming self-sufficient, and most importantly, they were being ministered to. My dad hired other staff and the local churches were our lifeline with respect to funding. We also came to the States a couple of times to raise funds. My brother and I traveled with our parents most of the time."

"Oh, you have a brother."

"Yes. He's three years older than I am. His name is Anthony. When I was sixteen my dad let me work in the office part-time and then full-time when I turned eighteen on days I was not at the university. My brother helped out as much as he could, but he wanted the law enforcement side of human trafficking. He became a police officer and eventually a detective. So, Anthony and I were at the center one day about four months after I started working full-time. We were closing the offices down when we heard a loud bang. I mean really loud."

"A gun?"

"We thought so. It was a truck that drove right through the metal fence. Immediately after is when we started hearing multiple gunshots. I remember my dad yelled out,'Ignacio!' Ignacio was my dad's assistant. They had an emergency plan in place in the event that something like this should happen. So I knew it was bad."

"Where was your mom?"

"She was getting in the car to go home. They shot and killed her." Marisol's voice was becoming softer.

"What about your dad?" he guardedly asked.

She turned her head to face him, fighting back the tears with everything she could. "No, he was shot and killed as well."

Felipe moved closer and gently put his arm around her. "I'm really sorry. You've probably heard that a million times, but I truly am." He had just met this girl, but everything in him wanted to comfort her.

"Thank you." She gently wiped the sides of her eyes with a napkin he handed her. "Well, I can tell you that my brother and I had an amazing upbringing," she added, trying to lighten the mood.

"Where is he now?"

Marisol felt her stomach recoil. "That's another long story. But I can't talk about this anymore tonight."

"No, of course not," he softly responded.

"I think I've given you enough drama for the remainder of the year."

"Hey, no judgments. I thought that was going to be like a rule with us. Friends don't judge each other."

"Okay, we're friends now instead of just neighbors," she responded as she blew her nose.

"I'd like to think we're on our way to becoming friends. Now I have two. You and Bernie."

She laughed at the simplicity with which he saw things. And she prayed that when he heard the rest of the story, he would still feel the same.

"Okay, friend. I have to open the discount store tomorrow super early, and I'm sure you have babies to deliver."

14

"Four days on, three off. That's my schedule. Just so you know. Listen, I know you must know a lot of people in this building."

"I have one friend and she lives down the hall. You know her."

"Who?"

"Fatima."

"She lives in this building and on this floor," he stated remembering the one time he had met Fatima, which had been at a hospital function.

"Be nice," Marisol smiled. "She's quirky, but an incredibly good friend."

"I didn't say anything," he said with a grin and happy that he was able to make her smile. "I just wanted you to know that if you ever need anything or just fire escape company, please call me."

"Right back at you and I appreciate it. But don't feel bad for me."

"Bad for you? I'm just looking for a way to collect on your turn for the wine." He winked at her and smiled, making her heart skip a beat.

"Buona notte, Felipe. Sogna con gli angeli." She winked back as she wished him a good night and sweet dreams.

"And you speak three languages."

"Yep," she called back from the inside of her bedroom.

* * *

La Esquinita Discount store sells beauty products, knick-knacks, and its biggest moneymaker, the pharmacy. It is owned by Rosa Gonzalez, the pharmacist, and Bernie's wife.

She is a middle-aged Cuban woman who is slightly taller than her husband. Short red hair and always immaculate, she has hazel eyes that sometimes take on a shade of light green, depending on the light. Like Bernie, she revalidated her credentials in America so she could work as a pharmacist. She liked the hours as they had allowed her to be there for Fatima when she attended school. Like her husband and daughter, she has a slight accent that she considers a badge of honor. She became a mother figure to Marisol.

The store never opens until ten a.m., but Marisol and Rosa always arrived early to prepare even when they worked on the occasional Saturday. Fatima worked on her days off from school.

"Someone looks tired," Rosa teased while she pulled meds out.

"Good morning. Me? Never," Marisol hoarsely replied sauntering in with her cup of coffee." She put her bag behind the counter and started setting up her display. "So I got to know my neighbor last night. He works with Bernie."

Rosa smiled. "Yes, Felipe Ortega. Bernie told me he moved in next door to you."

"He's going through a rough patch."

"Which of course pales in comparison to your story. How much did you share?" Rosa asked in a motherly tone.

"Well, enough that maybe he'll regret living next door to me."

"Not likely. He's nice. Bernie has been trying to get him to come to church, but he's been stubborn about it."

"Well, I have Fatima, but it's always nice to have one more friend. He grew up in church, but his church is way different than ours. He told me last night that even the people in the church were giving him a hard time over his breakup. I don't get that. Church is when you go when you're broken. No one talked about Jorje after he cheated on his wife."

"Well, most didn't. But people need to understand that no church is perfect. Mi hija, he has to realize that it's about having a relationship with Jesus, and only he can figure that out. You know what I mean?" she asked as she lightly tapped Marisol's nose.

"Amen. Ay Rosa, I believe with my heart and soul that my life is going to work itself out."

"Mama, God has a plan. We don't know which way he's going to roll, but he's got your situation under control."

The first customer walked in, and before they knew it, La Esquinita was buzzing with business.

* * *

A block away, Studio in the Heights was brimming with people getting in an early morning workout. Felipe had just gotten on the bike to begin warming up when Bernie took the one next to him.

"You come here often?" Bernie teased.

"Hey, what's going on? Did you just get here?"

"Yep. I walked Rosa to the discount and then got some coffee. I'm on call, but hopefully, it will be a quiet day and night."

"I'm out until Monday afternoon."

"Are you going to try to talk to your family this weekend?"

"No. I need to stay away for a while. Besides, it's important that I start making friends around here and I started last night. You weren't kidding when you said Marisol has been through a lot. I can't even imagine basically watching my parents get killed. She also mentioned she has a brother, but she got very emotional. I mean, who wouldn't? So she stopped."

"Give her time. She did the same with us. I could fill you in, but—"

"No, it needs to come from her."

"Exactly. It took a while before she opened up to us. Then Doña Tomasina died and—"

"Wait," Felipe interrupted out of breath. "Who's Doña Tomasina? I thought she lived alone?"

"Tomasina took her in and then she passed away. She'll tell you that story too."

"Incredible."

"And yet true."

The men continued the workout and stopped occasionally to chat.

* * *

The following Friday, Marisol was walking home from work when her phone buzzed.

Six p.m. fire escape. You owe me wine.

She smiled at Felipe's text. *That's thirty minutes from now. You bring cheese and crackers*, her delicate fingers responded. A nice cool shower washed off the day. She methodically did her hair in a French braid. Her grandmother had been a hairdresser in Honduras and each morning Marisol asked her to braid her hair for school. *I won't always be here to braid your hair,* she remembered her grandmother saying, and so she taught her how to do her own hair. She smiled at the memory as she sprayed herself with Sol De Oro Agua de Violetas, a cologne well known and used by Hispanics. Specifically made for babies, but used by women as well, it had a lavender refreshing scent. She put on a pair of black shorts and a light blue tank top.

She opened the window and as she stepped outside with the bottle of wine and two glasses, she noticed Felipe was already there in a black tank top and white shorts. He had set out a plate of cheese and crackers. *Jet black hair combed straight back, and of course, the infamous dimples that have all the women in the building swooning. That's going to be your trademark,* she thought as she casually sat down.

"There she is," Felipe greeted her.

Marisol spread out her quilt and handed him a glass. She had brought out a square piece of wood that she had found in the basement and used it as a flat surface on which to put the bottle.

"How are you?" she asked casually and with a smile.

"Good. You?"

"Okay," she responded as she started to pour the wine.

"What kind of wine did you bring?"

"It is a Merlot and I made it myself." She smiled and handed him the glass.

"Are you serious?"

"Yep. My Grandpa Vinnie, my dad's dad—my dad was named after him—taught my brother and me despite my dad asking him not to," she whispered as if not to get caught revealing a secret.

"Let me ask you something. If you were born in Honduras and lived there most of your life, how is it that you speak English so well?"

"Anthony, my brother, and I went to a bilingual school. I learned both languages at the same time. At home, we spoke both Spanish and English because my parents wanted us to really master both languages. My mom taught English at the center. My parents also made sure that we read a lot. And I mean a lot," she repeated widening her eyes. "My dad used to take us on vacation to Finca Las Glorias, which means—"

"I know," he interrupted. "Glorious Farms. You forget that I'm half Cuban."

"Discúlpame. My bad!"

"No worries," he smiled. "Go on."

"In English or Spanish?" she teased.

"Let's be consistent. Carry on in English." He winked.

She smiled as she felt her nose flutter. "Right, umm. Where was I?" she asked herself.

"Finca Las Glorias…" he said with a half-smile as he took another sip of wine.

"Right," she nodded."So we used to go there on vacation, and we rode horses, went swimming and even kayaking. My brother loved to draw and paint pictures of nature and created the most beautiful paintings. It's funny because he always signed his pictures, but he also included the emblem that looks like a fish, which stands for 'Jesus Christ, Son of God, Savior.'"

He nodded acknowledging.

"My mom used to say that if he ever went to America, he would become a popular artist." She smiled at the memory. "Then he went and got a degree in criminal justice and went into law enforcement. Being involved in the center in Honduras inspired a passion in him to fight human trafficking. He painted as a hobby. We were always involved in stuff. My dad also had a retreat for the women and children at the center and then a different one for the staff. So we were there a lot. Sometimes the power went out, but they were quick to restore it," she reminisced. "My parents made sure that all of us, not just me and my brother, but the women and children at the center as well had cultural experiences too. It was cool."

"How did you learn Italian?"

"Well, my grandparents on my dad's side did not speak English, so my dad taught us conversational Italian." She picked up a cracker and added cheese as he digested everything she had just told him.

"Honduras sounds like a beautiful place," he observed as he reached for a cracker himself.

"It is. We loved it. If what had happened had not happened, I'd still be there. I mean, don't get me wrong. I'm very grateful that I'm here, but I miss my country."

"I understand," he said warmly.

She took a deep breath knowing that she could put off the inevitable or just get it over with now. "I know that the missing piece is how I got to America. Are you ready?"

"No, are you ready to talk about it?" he asked sincerely.

"I am. I think the more I tell the story, the more I come to terms with it."

Chapter 3

"The afternoon my parents were killed, Anthony and I were driven to a location where two trucks were waiting for us. My brother was put on one and I was put in a separate one. We begged to be kept together, but they lied and told us the two trucks would be following each other. Three men were serving as guides or the people that took us through the journey. Some refer to them as coyotes. Other people were on the truck as well. So there was a total of four women including me. There were also two elderly men. As we made our way through Guatemala, we made several stops. They always made us sleep in barns and places where animals were kept. The stench of urine and feces was unbearable and pretty soon we started to smell like that. One morning, we were going through the mountains and I heard one of the guides tell the other guide 'the only one left to make our woman is the skinny one with the long hair,' which was me."

"What did you do?" Felipe cautiously asked.

"I jumped off the truck and ran," she said softly, "and thank God they didn't stop. They just kept going. I walked day and night for three days in the mountains of Mexico. I was bitten by a swarm of huge bees and my body started to swell. I had no food or water. The only thing I had on me was a brand-new bottle of Pepto Bismol that I found on the street before I got on the truck. One of the passengers told me I should throw it out, but something told me not to. There was also a lady on the truck who had given me a bunch of lemons, which I carried in my blouse. I know I fainted a few times, but each time I woke up, I asked God to give me strength. There were moments where I heard his voice audibly saying, 'Don't be afraid, for I am with you. Don't be discouraged, for I am your God. I will strengthen you and help you. I will uphold you with my righteous hand.'"

Isaiah 41:10, Felipe thought to himself.

"I sucked and ate the lemons and took small sips of the Pepto Bismol like it was water. At one point, I promised God that if I made it safely to the States, I would spend the rest of my life helping other people. On the last day that I was walking, a truck with four men slowed down. I had been walking with a stick as a cane because I could barely stand up. They asked me where I was going, and all I could do was stand there and cry. They asked me if I had been left by another group. All I did was cry. They said they would take me with them, and I was terrified, but I knew if I stayed, I would die. So I got in the truck and they placed me under their legs and covered me with a big coat." She took a sip of her wine for courage.

"When we got to Mexico City, they asked me if I had any money and I told them that I had left my money on the other truck. So they gave me one hundred Mexican pesos. It was enough so I could stay somewhere and make some phone calls. It's funny because these four guys looked like gangsters. They had small beady eyes and wore similar bandanas. If I had to guess, they probably were part of a gang. They were drinking and the conversations amongst themselves were clearly about drugs. But they did nothing but help me." Marisol's eyes were starting to pool with tears with Felipe following suit.

"One of them had a horrible nosebleed and I asked him if he would be okay if I put some lemon on his forehead. Hondurans use lemons to stop bleeding. So he allowed me to but was so respectful. He said something to me that I will never forget."

"What did he say?" Felipe asked.

She took a deep breath and looked straight into his eyes. "He told me that if I made it to the States, that I would do something wonderful with my life. I will never forget his face." Her voice broke as Felipe reached out and grabbed her hand in his.

"Do you want to stop?" he softly asked.

"No," she said as she blew her nose with the napkin he gave her. "I would rather finish now. So they dropped me off in Mexico City and I went into this small store. There was a young woman there looking at me. Of course, who could blame her? I was covered in blood and dirt. I had insect bites all over my body. I was sunburned so badly that my entire body had blistered and peeled really bad. My feet were totally and completely destroyed. My shoes actually disintegrated. I kept what little was left of them tied by ripping pieces of my shirt off for laces. My hair looked like a broom and I smelled sour. Like when you leave clothes in the washing machine for a few days? Anyway, she asked me if I wanted to go with her. She offered me a place to shower and a change of clothes. So

24

I went with her. I must have been in that shower for at least two hours. I had crusts of dirt in my hair and scalp." Marisol started tearing up again, but quickly regained her composure and continued.

"It felt so good to put on fresh clothes. She let me take a nap and then assisted me in locating a different guide. Again, I mounted a bus with about twenty other people, and then the task of crossing the border started. At one point we were told to get off and run. I ran so fast and fought so hard to get through the fence that my hair got tangled up and I had to yank it out. We crossed on foot and the truck picked us up on the other side. Then they traveled from state to state dropping people off. We made our way east until we got to New York. I was dropped off at Grand Central Station. We used to visit New York when my dad was itinerating for his ministry. Itinerating is what you do to raise money for your ministry."

"I know what itinerating is. Remember, I once went to church," he joked as he sipped his wine.

"That's right. I'm sorry."

He waved his hand indicating not to worry.

"There is a church here that we went to when we were in town. My dad made my brother and I memorize the address and phone number many years ago. We figured it was in case we got lost in this city while we were visiting. It was Sunday, so I gave the cab driver the address and by the grace of God, I got to the church during the last part of the service.

Pastor Juan Diaz loved my parents, but when I got to the church, he wasn't there anymore. He had taken a pastoral position in Columbia. I guess Pastor Melvin could see the fear on my face in hearing that the only person I knew was gone.

So he took me to his office. He made a few calls and found this place for me. Doña Tomasina was from Honduras too. Rosa was good friends with her. She agreed to take me in. Not long after that, she was diagnosed with cancer and she died a month later. She was the sweetest person ever."

Somehow, I think you're the sweetest person ever, he thought to himself as he looked at Marisol with nothing but admiration.

"Because she had lived in this building for so long, she qualified for rent control. She had known the super forever, so he let her pay the rent for the entire year after she was diagnosed. It's so funny because we worried about each other all the time. She was so good to me, especially those first few days after I got here." She sighed and continued. "Two weeks after I got here, there was a knock on the door. When I opened the door, there was a manilla envelope on the ground with my name on it."

"What was in it?"

"My passport stamped with the day I got here, a six-month tourist visa, my birth certificate, and the four pictures I had in the bag I had left on the first truck. No note. No return address. Nothing."

"That's insane."

"Tell me about it. So after Doña Tomasina passed away, Rosa hired me. Of course, off the books because I don't have a work permit."

"What happened to your brother?"

"I don't know. He could be anywhere. One thing is for sure, once my situation is taken care of, I'm going to find him."

"Can I ask you something?"

"Sure."

"How do you keep yourself together and smiling all the

time?"

She let out a small laugh and responded, "That's the easiest question I've ever been asked. I'm not alone. I've never been alone. God was with me with every drop of sweat and blood. Every step that I took when I was walking I knew was a step towards safety and freedom. God was there walking before me. I know that I'm okay now because I'm here. But when I was walking all those days after I jumped off that truck, I could feel his hand over me. So now things are uncertain, and I don't know what's going to happen. But I do know that I won't be alone. For some people, it's hard to have faith when they don't see a solution. I trust God with every part of my life. And, when my situation is solved, I will look for Anthony. Anyway, I'm ready to stop talking about this."

He knew to back off when she announced she was ready to move on. One of the things he liked about her was her complete transparency.

Marisol broke the serene silence. "So how many last week?" she asked, trying to lighten the mood. She was drained and it was the reason why she had only told her story twice. Once to Rosa, Bernie, Fatima, Doña Tomasina, and Pastor Melvin when they had gone to Rosa's for lunch one afternoon after church, and now Felipe.

"How many what?" he asked, still processing everything she had told him.

"How many babies?"

"Oh, too many," he laughed. "I did deliver my first set of twins and that was cool."

"Do you like working at Presbyterian?"

"I do. Someday I would love to open a practice right here. I love this neighborhood," he responded as he stared straight at the corner of Amsterdam Avenue. "Is that Fatima?"

Fatima Gonzalez is a younger version of her mother. Long hair to her waist, deep brown eyes with thick eyebrows, and thin as a rail, she carries herself as if she is Miss America. Just a few months older than Marisol, she was a third-year student at John Jay College of Criminal Justice. She is honest. Unpredictable. Loyal. And loud, showing off her deep Cuban accent. But that is Fatima, and as far as she is concerned, you can take her or leave her.

Marisol turned her head and saw Fatima walking toward the building with a smile and a thumbs up at the scenario before her. "Hey loca," she called out. "Come have some wine with us."

"By the way, this is really, really good," Felipe said about the wine.

"Oh, thank you," she said humbly. "It's not hard to make. You just have to be patient with the process."

"Can you show me how?"

"Are you patient enough?"

"I can be," he said as he looked deep into her eyes.

"Oye," Fatima screeched as she was toggling to get through the window and onto the fire escape. "This scene looks like it's right out of *West Side Story*." She stopped in her tracks when she saw Felipe. "Ay, but look who it is," she said with sophistication and then flipped a switch like she had seen an old buddy."Hey Felipe, what's up, man?"

"Not much. Hanging out with Marisol."

"I see, I see. And she opened one of her bottles for you. Ya tu sabes. Hey, you want to go for pizza? I don't cook on Fridays and it's already 7:30."

"Fatima, you never cook," Marisol reminded her.

"True. Pero, I do buy easy foods to make in the microwave. Bueno, are you people coming with me or not?" she asked as she stared at both of them.

"Sure," Marisol responded as she looked at Felipe.

"Where to, ladies? My treat."

Marisol turned around to face Fatima and mouthed the words, "Oh my God" as she pretended to be casually just looking at her friend.

"Let's go to Fresco's," Fatima suggested with a half-smile on her face.

They agreed to leave in half an hour.

* * *

Marisol showered again and was putting on fresh clothes while Fatima flipped through a magazine and sipped a glass of lemonade while sitting on her friend's bed.

"Oye, is it me, or was there a spark out there?" Fatima asked.

"I don't know what you're talking about," Marisol responded as she carefully applied her mascara.

"How much does he know?"

"He knows everything."

"Oh wow. Well, you got it over with. I remember when he started working at the hospital. I've seen him a couple of times. I don't remember what his specialty is, but I think he works in the ER with my dad. Oh, wait. He was doing his rotations then. Yeah, I don't remember," she added confused.

"He is an ob-gyn," Marisol informed her as she turned to find Fatima choking on her lemonade. "Are you okay?"

Fatima composed herself and started laughing uncontrollably. "Oh my God," she finally said after she got her breath.

"That is too funny. I'm sure you didn't tell him that part about you."

"Shhh," Marisol whispered.

"Marisol, there's no one here."

"These walls are thin," she continued to whisper. "Tell me in what universe that would be an appropriate conversation to have with a neighbor."

"He was looking at you like he wanted a little more," Fatima observed.

"I think it's all in your head."

"No, it's in my eyes."

"We've just met and become friends. Besides, you know that my time is ticking away." She spun around and looked at her friend as she smacked her lips together.

"Strawberry?" Fatima asked, referring to Marisol's choice of lip gloss.

"Cherry," she corrected her. Marisol felt her phone buzzing. *Are you ready?*

"That's Felipe and he's ready."

"Let's go," Fatima responded as she grabbed her purse.

He was already downstairs when Marisol and Fatima came out of the building. She was walking toward him, and he was taking note of her cute shape and walk. Her smile was enough to light up a room and automatically made him smile.

"I can't believe we are halfway through August," Fatima pointed out since she was eagerly anticipating the fall.

"Don't you have that seminar coming up?" Marisol asked.

"Si, I leave a week from Sunday. I want to be there the night before. It's at the University of New Haven and it's only for two days," she responded.

"What kind of seminar?" Felipe asked.

"It's on criminal justice ethics." She rolled her eyes. "I'm just so tired of going to school when I know that as soon as I graduate, I'm going to enroll in the police academy."

"You might change your mind after you graduate," Marisol said.

They got to the pizza place and Felipe held the door open for them to walk through. He couldn't help but catch the sweet, lavender-clean scent that emanated from Marisol.

She made sure to get the seat facing the door. Felipe sat next to Marisol, and Fatima seated herself opposite both.

"Let's get a large pizza," Fatima suggested.

"That's fine with me," Marisol agreed.

"What do you want on it? I like everything on it, but we can get half and half," Felipe said.

"Okay, let's get half with everything and half with ham?" Marisol looked at Fatima.

"That's fine with me," Fatima said as she took out her gum and placed it in her paper napkin. "Hey, when are we going to squeeze the juice out of the grapes?" she asked Marisol.

"Actually, I have a few containers that are ready. Tomorrow?"

"What are you talking about?" Felipe asked.

"Chico, the juice from grapes for the wine," Fatima responded.

"You wanted to learn how to make wine. I went through this whole lesson with Fatima last week, but you can join us if you want to. It's the more hands-on time of the process. I mean, if you're not busy."

He smiled as the pizza was being placed in front of them. "I have nothing to do tomorrow, and it sounds like it would be fun. Count me in."

Fatima, who had her reading glasses on the bridge of her

nose, looked at Felipe. Then at Marisol. Back at Felipe. And then again at Marisol before mumbling, "Ay Dios mio."

They ate as they talked about the weather, a trip to Jones Beach before the end of summer, and of course the upcoming block party. They chatted away until Felipe noticed an interesting pattern developing on Marisol's plate.

"What's wrong?" Marisol asked Felipe who was looking at her plate.

She had systematically eaten everything but the crust. Felipe had been staring at the collection of log crusts she had accumulated on her plate and then watched her dip each one in the sauce that came with the bread.

"Oh, that's how she eats pizza," Fatima explained when she looked at Marisol's plate.

"I can see that," he said.

"The ends are dry, so I eat them separately so I can dip them," she smiled as she bit into one.

Could she possibly *get any cuter?* he wondered. He paid for their meal and they walked back to the building.

* * *

"Okay, so I need everyone at my apartment by ten a.m.," Marisol instructed them as they were getting in the elevator to go up to their floor.

"Okay, boss," Fatima responded.

"The commute is short, so no problem," Felipe joked.

Each went to their door like children going to their rooms seeking their beds for slumber.

Heavenly Father, Marisol began as she lay in bed, *I come to you in complete and total thanksgiving for my health, this apartment, and the food I have in my refrigerator. Thank you for each of the people in my life that make a difference. You tell us 'Come to me, all of you who are weary and carry heavy burdens, and I will give you rest. Take my yoke upon you. Let me teach you because I am gentle and humble at heart, and you will find rest for your souls. For my yoke is easy to bear, and the burden I give you is light.' Lord, I cling to your word. And I know that no matter how terrible things look, you are going to take care of me. Please send me a miracle to put this situation out of my life once and for all.* Her eyes were getting heavy, and as she said, a*men,* she fell asleep.

Chapter 4

Marisol was up by five a.m. with a cup of coffee out on the fire escape to do her devotional. She could feel the difference in the temperature as if August knew it was almost time to bow out and for fall to take center stage. It made her wonder if it looked the way she had seen in pictures. She had only visited the States with her family in the spring. She put her cup down and opened her One Year Bible. A chapter from the Old Testament, one from the New Testament, a psalm, and a proverb—that was the recipe for her daily reading. Then she just sat and meditated on what she had read.

Marisol made some more coffee and took a shower. She put on her beat-up jeans with a T-shirt and gathered her hair in a ponytail. A little eyeliner, some lip gloss, and she was ready to go. She started by sorting through some more grapes. Taking off the stems, throwing away tainted berries or berries with mold became her mission, and she was focused. She had done it so many times that she was going at the speed of lightning and was done in one hour.

The wine room had three long wooden tables that were placed on each side of the room with four huge enamel wine storage barrels underneath. She had a portable plastic bin with multiple drawers where she kept clean cloths, dish rags, corks, and other tools. A portable sink that Doña Tomasina had installed a few days after Marisol arrived was against a shared honey-colored bathroom wall.

Marisol made sure everything was in place and started a fresh pot of coffee.

"Good morning," Felipe said as he walked through the door and hugged her, picking up that clean, lavender scent that she wore so well.

"Good morning," she returned the greeting with a smile.

"Your apartment is similar to mine."

"Come, I'll show you around. So that room to the right is the wine room. That's where we are going to work." She proceeded to show him the rest of the apartment, and then before they went into the kitchen to have coffee, Marisol turned the radio on to a station that played oldies.

"Have you talked to your family?" she carefully asked as she poured him a cup.

"No, I'm going to see them next Saturday."

"Well, you've had a chance to cool off and so have they. I'm sure it will go well."

"We'll see."

"Hey! I'm here!" Fatima announced as she walked down the hall and into the kitchen.

She plopped a box of donuts in the center of the table. "I brought these so we could eat something before we start."

Marisol poured her some coffee, and after they ate their

donuts, they were ready for duty.

"Okay," Marisol started as Felipe and Fatima stood by waiting for directions."Today we are going to mash the grapes. This is done with either a wooden spoon or your hands."

"I call the wooden spoon," Fatima announced.

"That's fine. I use my hands because we don't want to damage the seeds. If the grapes become overprocessed, they release too much tannin, which will give the wine a bitter taste."

Felipe and Fatima stared at her like she was speaking in another language.

"Excuse me, pero, what is tannin?" Fatima inquired.

"It's a compound in the grape skins, seeds, and stems."

"Oh," the other two said in unison.

"So Felipe, you will help me, and Fatima, since you want to use the wooden spoon, you take the first barrel." Fatima picked up the wooden spoon and started gently mashing the grapes.

Marisol went back to the living room. She shut off the stereo, took the big portable boombox and placed it in the kitchen with the same station. They had an Elton John special going on and Marisol wanted them to be able to hear.

"Hey, you left me," Felipe teased.

"No, I was getting the music closer. Did you wash your hands?"

"Yes, I did. It's kind of like scrubbing in for surgery." He smiled as he watched her wash her hands.

"Here we go," she said as she buried her hands in the grapes.

Felipe was standing right over in proximity and he could smell the residue of the coconut shampoo on her hair. She was looking into the bucket as she managed the grapes and he noticed that she had long, extraordinary, silky eyelashes.

Half an hour had gone by when he asked, "Am I doing this right?"

Marisol's hands made their way over for inspection and she felt her heartbeat increase as she placed her hands on his to guide him. She couldn't help but notice how strong his hands felt. Full of confidence and security. She looked up at him and felt her knees go weak.

"You're doing this just perfect," she said as she smiled.

Their trance was broken by Fatima. "Oye, I need a break."

"Yes, Fatima, go. Take a break," Marisol instructed as she continued her grape-smashing dance with Felipe.

"Is there anything you don't know how to do?" he teased.

Oh My God. If you only knew, she thought. "Oh, there's many things." They were looking deeply into each other's eyes until they heard a noise that sounded like drowning cats.

"Hold me close, Tonyyyyy Daaanza," Fatima belted from the kitchen as she sang along totally off-key to Elton John's "Tiny Dancer."

Felipe looked at Marisol and said, "Did she mean 'hold me close, tiny dancer'?"

Marisol nodded and they both started laughing.

"Fatima," Marisol yelled as she was still laughing.

"What?" she yelled back.

"Come on. You have to get this done."

"On my way." They heard her making her way back into the room. "Oye, that Elton John is amazing."

"Yes, he is," Marisol said. "Look at you go," she said directing her comment to Felipe who was gently squeezing away at the grapes.

"I'm glad you asked me to come help."

"Me too," she responded sweetly.

They continued working until all the grapes were properly mashed.

"Okay, before we do anything else," Marisol instructed, "we have to wash our hands with soap and hydrogen peroxide. I made a small mix this morning. Then we are going to cover the containers."

They proceeded to wash their hands and Marisol even gave them small brushes to scrub with. She pulled clean special cloths from the bin and they covered each container.

"Now we have to cover them for three to four days. In about twelve to twenty hours the juice will begin to ferment. I have to come in here a couple of times a day to do something to it, but it doesn't take long. You both helped me a lot today."

"That's it?" Fatima asked, disappointed.

"I told you that it takes patience and time," Marisol responded as she dried her hands with the dishtowel.

"I guess," she responded.

"In a few weeks, we'll be drinking the wine you helped make," she reassured them, not realizing how drastically her life would change by then.

By the time they had finished cleaning up and leaving the room organized at Marisol's insistence, it was almost two p.m. The rest of the weekend and the following week went by with Felipe working a few overnight shifts. Fatima was busy with school and Marisol had met with a local immigration attorney.

* * *

"You have to get someone that's really good," Fatima said to Marisol on Thursday when she stopped by for coffee after dinner.

"You know that I can't afford a fancy attorney. This guy is good. It's just that my situation is complicated because there is a lot that I can't tell him. So it's taking him longer to find the proper option for me."

"Where did you find him?" Fatima protectively asked.

"It's that new place on the corner. They just opened up, but the guy sounded like he could help me."

"Marisol, your case is complicated. You need someone that knows what they're doing. We've offered to help you pay—"

Although she knew that Fatima meant well, she had struck a nerve. "I know you have," she said, gently placing her hand on her friend," but everyone has their own problems. Can you imagine how I would feel if I took money from your family and then I got sent back? I couldn't live with that, Fatima. I don't know who sent me those documents, but you know that if anyone found out that I crossed the border without them, it would be fraud."

"You are family, mama," she gently said as she put her hand on hers. "You're running out of time. You know you can't go back. What does Felipe say?"

"He's offered to help me as well, but I've got this. I love you for caring so much, but I'm an adult. I've got this."

"I know that you have experienced more than most people do in an entire lifetime, but you just turned twenty-one."

"I'll be fine. Please don't worry. These things take time, and we just have to be patient." Marisol heard her phone vibrate on the counter.

Stopping at Gristede's to get a couple of things. Want anything?

She smiled at his chivalry. There wasn't a time that he stopped at the market or the corner bodega and did not text to ask if she needed anything. *No, thank you though!*

"Let me guess. Felipe," Fatima said matter of factly as she crossed her arms.

"Huh?" Marisol looked up smiling, not even sure of what Fatima had just said.

"Ay mi madre. Oye, you like el médico, don't you?"

"We've become good friends," Marisol said as she stood up to stir the arroz con pollo.

"My dad says you're cooking for him," she teased.

"No, I've been giving him food when I cook too much. I do the same with you."

"Yes, but I don't tell anyone that will listen with a smile from ear to ear," Fatima informed her.

Marisol turned her attention back to the pot and smiled as she continued to stir.

"He told my dad when they were eating dinner at the hospital the other night. My dad was surprised to see him eating a homemade meal. So when he commented on it, he said that Felipe turned red and was smiling telling him you had given it to him."

"Well, I give you food and tonight I'm taking some of this," Marisol said as she pointed to the pot, "to Mercedes. She hasn't been feeling well."

"The old lady on the fifth floor? Okay, but tell me this," Fatima challenged, "how are you going to dress to take it to her?"

"Shorts and a T-shirt. What else?"

"So you're not going to wear your cute white shorts with the black tank and matching sandals?"

"When have you ever seen me wear that around here?"

"Uh, the other day when you went to get the mail and Felipe

just happened to be coming home from work."

She opened her mouth to refute her friend's allegations and then remembered. "Well, it's nice to dress up once in a while," she embarrassingly admitted. "Yes, I think he's attractive, but we're just friends."

"I think you should go for it," Fatima casually said as she filed her nails.

"I don't think so," Marisol replied just as casually.

"You're an adult. You're really going to wait until you get married?"

"You know what I think?" Marisol said desperately trying to change the conversation.

"What?" Fatima eagerly listened hoping Marisol was reconsidering.

"I think I need to go shower, so I can take this food up to Mercedes."

"You're too much. Okay, I need to go anyway," she replied looking at the time.

"Date tonight?" Marisol teased.

"No, I'm going to go color Graciela's hair. My mother's neighbor."

"Again?" Marisol exclaimed.

"Mi hija, she changes colors every month."

"What color is she doing now?"

"Get this. Red, white, and blue. She just became a citizen and says it is her civic duty to show gratitude."

Marisol smiled longingly. She would be coloring her hair that way too if she could just get her immigration status resolved.

Fatima knew what she was thinking and said, "I'm sorry. I shouldn't have brought up that, vieja."

"No, it's okay. Don't be silly. You better go."

"I'll call you when I get home. We can maybe watch an episode of *Caso Cerrado*."

"Sounds good."

* * *

It was around 8:30 when Marisol got into the elevator after visiting Mercedes for an hour. She loved Marisol's chicken and rice, and each time she cooked, she always remembered to take some to the elderly lady. She got on the elevator, pressed two, leaned back, and closed her eyes, making a mental list of things to do. Suddenly, the elevator stopped with a thump. She tried to press the "open door" button to no avail. Marisol started to smell smoke.

Covering for another doctor, Felipe had worked a midshift and was turning onto St. Nicholas Avenue when he saw two fire trucks and an ambulance on the street that was also flooded with neighbors dressed in pajamas or whatever they could get on before evacuating. Neighbors in the surrounding buildings also came out. He ran toward the crowd and frantically searched for Marisol. He spotted Fatima.

"Where is Marisol?" he asked out of breath.

"I wasn't home. I was across the street and saw all the commotion, so I came out and started looking for her. She was going to Mercedes' apartment to give her—" Fatima stopped talking when she saw the elderly woman being led away from the building. Felipe followed her as she ran toward Mercedes.

"Doña Mercedes, adónde está Marisol? Did she bring you food?" Fatima nervously asked.

"Si, pero she left about five minutes before this happened."

Felipe and Fatima looked at each other and they knew. "She's stuck in the elevator," he said as he hurried past the crowd, taking the stairs two by two. Since he was dressed in scrubs, no one bothered to stop him.

Doing some calculations and talking to the firefighters, they figured she had to be stuck between the third and second floors.

"Marisol, can you hear me?" Felipe screamed.

"Yes, there's smoke coming in slowly," she said coughing.

"I'm here with the firefighters. We're on it." After struggling for a few minutes with a specialized tool, four firefighters and Felipe managed to open the door. The elevator was stuck, and Marisol would have to jump a long distance to get out.

"Ma'am, you're going to have to come down," the firefighter instructed.

You don't know how strong and fearless this lady is, Felipe thought as he looked at the firefighter. He stepped forward. "Marisol, come on. I got you. Just lean over and I'll grab you," he calmly said.

She sat on the floor with her legs dangling out and reached out her arms until Felipe grabbed her as if he were picking up a child. Losing his balance, he fell back with Marisol on top of him.

"We have to stop meeting like this," he said out of breath but with a smile.

He felt her light body squirming to get off him and she could feel her cheeks getting hot, although she was grateful that she could blame it on the fire.

"Thank you so much," she said. After making sure she was okay, they hurried out of the building.

Bernie, Rosa, Fatima, and all the neighbors were outside.

"Ay mi hija, they wouldn't let us come inside, but we knew they had let Felipe in," Rosa said as she went and hugged Felipe. "Gracias, mi hijo," she kept repeating.

"No hay de que," he said, assuring her that there was no need to thank him.

"You okay?" he asked Marisol again.

"I'm fine," she replied as her nose convulsed.

"Liar," he responded already noticing her body language when she was nervous.

"Thank you, again."

"Who was going to make wine for me if I didn't get you out of there?" he said, looking deeply into her eyes.

"Oye," Fatima called out to Marisol. "You won't believe who it was. Anastacio el Apestoso set the trash in the basement on fire. I knew we were due any day."

Marisol looked at Felipe who was looking at Fatima totally perplexed.

"Anastacio never showers, hence the nickname el Apestoso. He got divorced about five years ago and on the anniversary of his divorce, he sets the trash in the basement on fire," Marisol said explaining the history of the culprit's deed.

"How do you know all this?" he asked.

"Doña Tomasina told me one night. I just forgot to mark it on the calendar. She told me people often knew and planned around it. How sad is that?"

The crowds that lived in the building across the street, which included Bernie and Rosa, had gone home when the firefighters assured the residents of the building that it was perfectly safe to go back inside although the elevator would be out of commission for a few days.

"Bueno gente," Fatima announced to Marisol and Felipe as

44

they made their way up the stairs. "I'm going to hit the pack."

"Hit the sack," the other two said in unison as they each entered their apartments calling it a night.

Chapter 5

T he following Saturday came faster than Felipe had anticipated. Walking to work and taking the train made having a car in the city an inconvenience. At least that's what he was telling himself. But he knew that he needed to start making amends with his mother. Dropping off the car at home was a convenient excuse to go visit.

He sat in the driveway for what seemed like an hour. It would be the first time Felipe would see his family since the breakup with Sandra and the drive to Connecticut had prepared him for the conversation.

"Bro!" Alex pulled his older brother in and hugged him. "What's happening, man? How's the city treating you?"

"Good, good. You have to come and visit me soon."

"Visit? I'm starting to look for an apartment down there because the commute is getting stressful."

"It is stressful. I'll keep an ear out in case anything comes up. Would you mind living way uptown?"

"Nah. Not at all," Alex said as they approached the family

room.

So much had happened since the last time Felipe had been home that he felt like a stranger in the house where he had been raised. He hugged his parents and sat in the recliner he had claimed as his since high school.

Felipe broke the silence. "So I thought it would be good for us to talk. I don't want things to be strained for us."

"You left your fiancé high and dry. Felipe, we raised you better. How could you do this?" his mother questioned.

"Mom, would you have wanted me to marry Sandra at the expense of being unhappy?"

"You couldn't have figured it out sooner? This was not some girl you had been casually seeing."

"Victoria," Felipe Sr. sharply interrupted, "we said we would not do this."

"No Dad, it's okay. Let's get this all out."

"You were both accepted into Harvard and Yale," Victoria continued without missing a beat. "Sandra wanted Harvard. Would it have killed you to go there? Residency comes up and she applies in Connecticut. You decide you want the city. I don't understand you."

"No, Mom. You just don't understand. We wanted different things. It wasn't just about geography. Sandra is a wonderful woman with great qualities, but her interest in becoming a doctor was making money."

"So what's wrong with that?" Victoria retorted.

He stared at her incredulously and responded, "Because that's not why I became a doctor."

"You deliver babies, and you can do that anywhere. My church friends said that—"

"Seriously?" her son interrupted. "Mom, that's one of the

reasons why I stopped going to church."

"No, you stopped going because the congregation—"

"Okay, ya basta. Enough," Felipe Sr. sternly interrupted. "Mi hijo, how's it going in Washington Heights?"

Victoria rolled her eyes and sat back at her husband's subtle attempt to change the conversation.

"Hold on, Dad," Felipe respectfully addressed his father. "Mom," he said redirecting himself to his mother," I don't care what people in the church are saying. This is not a movie or a soap opera. This is my life and whatever decisions I make now, whether you think they are selfish or not, are mine. I have to live with them. And Sandra, I heard she's already seeing someone else, so she couldn't have been that devastated." He abruptly turned to his father and continued. "Dad, I have a few close friends. I can take the train to work, and the hospital I'm working in is the best. I have phenomenal colleagues."

He glanced over at his mother, who had started filing her nails. She knew how far to push the Ortega men before they pushed back. And when they did, the discussion was over. But she still plunged ahead with one other agenda item that she had pending.

"There's one more thing I want to tell you," Victoria said as she put her nail file on the end table. "You know the property my mother left you was yours with one stipulation."

"What stipulation?" Felipe asked confused.

"That property would become yours once you got married."

"You're not going to let this go, are you?" he responded in a cold voice.

"I'm just telling you that's what was in my mother's will."

"You know what? That's fine."

"She left it for you to open up a practice here in town,"

48

Victoria responded.

"So let me see if I understand this. Nona left me the property with no access to it until I got married and with the request that I open up a practice here. That's ridiculous. But you know what? That's fine. I don't need it."

"Bueno, let's have lunch," Felipe Sr. announced as a way of saying the conversation of money and material things was over. Once the family sat at the table for a meal, there was to be zero arguing. It was a family standard that he had established when the boys were young.

The conversations became lighter as they ate lunch. The upcoming football season kept the men talking for a good twenty minutes, while Victoria looked bored.

"What about the building you live in?" his mother asked as a way to bring up a topic in which she could participate.

"What about it?" Felipe asked confused.

"How do you like it?" she asked with a softer tone.

"It's great." Something deep down inside urged him not to say anything more. Not because he was ashamed of Marisol. But because he had become very protective of her and would swing at anyone who dared say one word about her. "The people are really down to earth and I'm starting to get a lot of Spanish recipes, so look out, Dad."

Felipe said goodbye to his parents, and since he was leaving his car at the house, his brother drove him to the train station.

"Thank you for dropping me off, bro. You have to come visit me soon. I have a spare room. That way you can check out the building," Felipe said as he hugged his brother goodbye.

"For sure. We'll make that happen soon. You did the right thing about Sandra."

"Yeah, I know you didn't like her very much."

"Didn't matter what I thought. I just wanted you to be happy and you weren't. Mom's gonna come around. You know that when things don't go her way, her go-to strategy is to push back."

"Yeah, I know." They hugged each other again and Felipe got on the train.

What are you doing? he texted Marisol once he was settled in his seat.

Watching a Friends marathon. LOL. How did it go?

Meh. It could have gone better. Fire escape in about 2.5 hours? Your turn for wine.

Not homemade for sure, but I do have a competitive brand.

Sounds good to me. I made sandwiches.

Oooo. Fancy! See you soon.

* * *

"It couldn't have been that bad." She took her glass of wine as was customary and gave him a sandwich as they settled themselves on the fire escape.

"Wanna bet? It's not so much my dad and my brother, but my mom is another story. She's so hung up on how bad the whole thing looked for the church and how I hurt Sandra, and of course, there was the whole 'you are so selfish' sonata." She listened quietly as he had done with her. "Somehow, my mother thinks I have an ulterior motive for everything I do."

"Do you think you do?"

"I don't think so but she's told me so often I'm starting to doubt myself."

"It sounds like you weren't at peace with marrying Sandra."

"You sound like my brother," he responded as he let out a

slight laugh.

"What is she like?"

"Who? Sandra?"

"Yeah."

"She's beautiful, decent, smart. But we just don't want the same things. It's really that simple. When I think about it, she's a lot like my mom in a way. She always worried about what people would say and she lived our entire relationship like it was a storybook. That's why she wanted us to build our practices in Connecticut and live in the suburbs. Have a few kids, who of course would all be perfect."

"Is that how you grew up?"

"My parents didn't come into money the way hers did. My dad built a business in real estate from the ground up. I was able to go to an Ivy League school because of that. My mother came from Italy to New York when she was a teenager, and my dad came from Cuba when he was two. So he had lived in the States longer than my mom when they met in high school. All four of my grandparents struggled when they came to this country, but they made it through. My dad got over it, but I don't think my mom ever did. You know, being poor. She went to school of course and became a nurse, but she always has that fear of having nothing. So she constantly chases after material things."

"It's not easy. Well, give your mom some time. It hasn't been that long, and some people take a longer time to process stuff. Must have been nice to see your brother."

"Yes, it was," he smiled. "He's commuting right now and getting fed up with it. I asked him to come visit soon so he can check out this neighborhood. Maybe while he's here I can talk to him about your sit—"

Marisol didn't even let him finish "I truly appreciate it, but I can't."

"He's my brother," Felipe said. "He's not going to charge you anything."

Marisol sighed. "Okay, let's compromise. If I don't hear anything from the attorney at that center I went to, then you tell Alex about my situation."

Imagine that. A compromise. Something Sandra would have never done, Felipe thought before he said, "You are so stubborn."

"Of course, I am," she said with a smile as she shifted positions.

"So let me ask you something. You told me that you worked at the center in Honduras, on the days you weren't at the university. What were you majoring in?"

"I started taking courses at Universidad de San Pedro Sula. I wanted to be a court reporter."

"Why a court reporter?"

"I wanted to work in a courtroom, and when you're a court reporter, you get to hear all kinds of interesting cases." But she continued introspectively, "Maybe I would have gone to law school." She snapped out of her deep thought and added, "I was a great student!"

"I bet you were. I also bet you had a lot of guys running after you."

"Moi?"

"Let me guess. You speak French too."

"Not really. It's the only thing I know how to say. I had a lot of friends and dated this one guy for a couple of months, but it wasn't easy. We had too much security and he just got tired of having to go through Fort Knox just to see me."

"His loss completely."

"Thank you," she responded shyly. "Hey, I know tomorrow is day three of your four days on three days off cycle."

"You're keeping track," he smiled.

"I have a thing with calendars and dates. Anyway, I've hinted around before, but I'm just going to ask you outright. That's what friends do."

"Go for it." *I know she's going to ask me to go to church again.*

"You had a tough day today and those feelings can really take a toll."

"You'd make a great lawyer. You're stating your case."

"Of course. As I was saying, confrontations can leave you drained, and once you get back inside, you know you're going to mull over everything that happened today and think God knows what. So I think you should come to church with me tomorrow." He sighed and she was waiting for the no he was just about to throw at her again.

Remembering the conversation he had just had with his mother and why he had stopped going to church, he decided to take a chance. If the people who lived in the neighborhood are the ones who attended that church, he knew that perhaps he might find what had been missing in Connecticut.

"You are quite persuasive, so I will go to church with you tomorrow."

"Really?" she smiled. "I thought I was going to have to resort to the second argument."

"Which was?"

"No more homemade wine for you."

* * *

Marisol lay wide awake in her bed. *Heavenly Father, please meet*

Felipe where he is. I pray that you bring peace to his soul and that you touch his family with that same spirit. Let him see that there is nothing more wonderful in this life than having a relationship with you. You have given him the gift of bringing life into this world and having a relationship with you would just be the best thing ever. Bless Anthony, wherever he may be, and somehow let him know that as soon as my problems are solved, I will look for him. I love you, Jesus.

* * *

A slight wind blew the curtain and on the other side of the wall lay Felipe staring straight at the ceiling. And for the first time in a long time, the words came. *Hey God. It's me. Felipe. I know it's been years. But Marisol says that we should run to you and not be away from you. I'm really mad at my mom and I don't know how to handle it. Maybe going to church tomorrow will help. It couldn't hurt. That's for sure.* Again, the cool midnight breeze blew his curtain, and he was asleep before he knew it.

Chapter 6

La Iglesia de Esperanza Y Victoria is one of a few churches that serves the Christian community in Washington Heights, and its warmth and familial environment is what keeps the steady number of parishioners in attendance each week. One of the changes Pastor Melvin Hernandez implemented since taking the position of Senior Pastor was to have services in both Spanish and English, which was successful in bringing in the younger generation. Through the worship set, Felipe could hear Marisol hitting high notes, which more than likely pegged her as a soprano. Morning announcements were made, the offering was collected, and the service began.

"We are all different people with different experiences," Pastor Melvin plunged right in, "but there are many experiences that we can consider common. For example, a broken promise, a shattered dream, and even an expectation that never comes to pass. Solomon, who was King David's son, wrote about his own disappointments and he tried to find peace away from God. In the second chapter of Ecclesiastes, he records a series of examples, such as wealth, wisdom, popularity, and pleasure and how each of them ends in disappointment if it becomes the sole reason for our existence. Throughout the chapter, he works through these scenarios and comes to the final conclusion, 'fear God and obey his commands, for this is everyone's duty.' And I need to clarify that the word 'fear' does not mean afraid or trembling." The congregation laughed as Pastor Melvin shook as if scared. "It means respect, reverence, and awe."

Felipe couldn't help but notice how Marisol had her Bible color-coded with notes on almost every page. She placed the book on both their laps, which only made them sit closer. She could smell the Grey Flannel cologne. He put his arm around the back of her chair so he could lean into the book.

Marisol's heart was thumping, and she was convinced he could hear it as she nonchalantly smiled. *Okay. Be cool,* she instructed herself.

Pastor Melvin read verses 1-9 and then surmised, "So here we have Solomon telling us in verse 9 'Let's look for the good things in life. But I found this too was meaningless.' He continues by 'trying to build a huge home,' verse 4. In verse 7, he talks about 'the large flocks,' and in verse 8, he describes how he 'hired wonderful singers, both men and women, and had many beautiful concubines.'" At the word concubines, Felipe heard Marisol, whisper, "Oh, Lord," under her breath as she uncomfortably shifted her position. He made a mental note to ask her about that later. He turned his gaze back to Pastor Melvin.

"And it's in verse 9 where he delivers his revelation. 'So I became greater than all who had lived in Jerusalem before me, and my wisdom never failed me. Anything I wanted; I would take. I denied myself no pleasure in hard work, a reward for all my labors. But, as I looked at everything, I had worked so hard to accomplish, it was all so meaningless – like chasing the wind. There was nothing really worthwhile anywhere.' Brothers and sisters, we all want a better life and there is nothing wrong with that, but we have to make sure that what we are fighting for is the people in our lives and that the dreams that we go after have a fruitful meaning. Think about it."

* * *

The foyer was buzzing with people buying things in the gift shop and deciding where to have lunch. Rosa approached Marisol, Felipe, and Fatima.

"Bernie and I want to treat everyone to La Nueva España. But we need to get going because that place fills up fast," she announced in her matriarch voice. The five of them walked the three blocks down St. Nicholas Avenue.

"Table for five?" the hostess asked.

"Yes, please," Bernie responded.

The server looked around and realized there were no booths available. "I don't have any booths available. Is this table okay?" she asked.

Bernie turned to get a consensus from the group. "Do you want to wait for a booth?"

"I'm fine with a table, Bernie. You know I'm not too picky," Marisol replied.

The others agreed and they settled down at their table.

"Hi, I'm Jose and I'm going to be your server." Jose proceeded to take everyone's order smoothly and then he got to Marisol.

"And I will have the Bistec Empanizado with white rice, but I want the black beans strained and on the side. Oh, and maduros. Also, can I get an extra plate and a box so I can split up my meal?"

Felipe stared at her with a slight grin on his face.

Marisol picked up her napkin and noticed he was staring. "What? Do I have something on my face?" she questioned as she rubbed her face.

"No, I was just marveling at your directions for the server."

"Well, I just like things the way I like them."

"I noticed that with the pizza crust," he teased.

Impressed that he had remembered her idiosyncrasy with pizza, she smiled and delicately took a piece of bread from the basket. With their food orders taken, they started debriefing the service.

"I think about what the pastor says all the time," Fatima kicked off as she buttered a piece of bread. "Think about it. Look at all the things we are always buying, and do they really bring up happiness? No. Not even a woman made Solomon happy even though he thought so at the time."

"Speaking of women," Felipe taunted Marisol, "what was up with that comment you made after the pastor talked about concubines?"

"This is going to be fun," Fatima chimed in as Bernie and Rosa smiled.

"Seriously? Let's take a look at the Old Testament starting with Adam and Eve," Marisol challenged.

"Ay Dios, here we go," Rosa interjected. Marisol looked over at her and then straight at Felipe.

"Eve offers Adam the apple and he takes it. When God comes looking for them, Adam blames all the events on Eve. Sarah can't have children so she asks Abraham to sleep with Hagar so they can have a child, and of course, he makes the ultimate sacrifice and sleeps with her. If that isn't bad enough, men in the Old Testament had multiple wives." Her eyes widened, and Felipe couldn't help but notice how big and beautiful they were.

"Are you sorry you asked?" Fatima broke his concentration as he decided to stir things up with Marisol.

"Well, it was Eve that gave Adam the apple, right?"

"Oye, are you trying to add, como se llama, fuel to the smoke?"

"Fuel to the fire," Rosa and Bernie said in unison.

"He knows what I meant," Fatima said.

"Si, pero learn to say it right," her father replied.

"It's okay, Fatima. I've got this," Marisol said ignoring the exchange between Fatima and her parents.

"He could have been a real man and said no," Marisol said directly to Felipe.

"So you're saying that Eve was weak, and she needed Adam to put his foot down," he countered intending to watch her become exasperated with him.

"No! I'm saying that he needed to take responsibility as opposed to saying, 'she did it.'"

"Oye," Bernie broke the debate. "No hablen más disparates. The food is here."

Before she started eating, she split her meal evenly into two parts, knowing that now she had a decent dinner for two days. Rosa said grace and they dug into their meals.

Marisol rubbed her belly as if she had eaten her meal completely. "I'm so full," she complained.

"Flaca, you need to eat more," Bernie countered with a

mouth full of flan. She couldn't blame him for saying that. She never let on to anything that went past her front door and that included that sometimes she had to settle for sandwiches or wine and cheese.

"I'm working on it. I need to go home and take a nap. I woke up with a slight headache. I took something for it, and it went away, but I'm starting to feel it again."

"I meant to tell you yesterday that you look tired. Do you want to take tomorrow off?" Rosa questioned with a voice of concern.

"Of course not. I'll be fine," she lied. "But I think I'm going to get going."

"Me too." Felipe started to go for his wallet.

Bernie saw his intention and said, "No, I already said today was on me. Next time you treat. What time do you start tomorrow?"

"I'm on from two p.m. to midnight. What about you?"

"No, I'm leaving in a couple of hours with Rosa. We're going to New Jersey for the day because Rosa has a conference and I'm going to see my brother. We'll be back tomorrow afternoon, but I promised my brother we would come in tonight."

"Nice," Felipe responded.

They said their goodbyes and Felipe and Marisol started walking home. He could see that Marisol's energy was low.

* * *

"Are you sure you're okay?" he asked as they approached the building.

"I'm fine. They worry too much. I'll prove it to you. As

soon as I get up from my nap, we'll have some wine on the fire escape." She made light of the situation, but he could tell she was struggling.

"I've been meaning to ask you about that. In a week, it will be September and it will soon start to get cooler. We need to find a different place for our wine drinking escapades."

She smiled at the word escapades. "I guess we can take turns. You're always welcome in my apartment."

"You make good wine, but I'm a great cook! Remember, we both have Italian and Hispanic in us, and of course, there's the fact that men are just better chefs," he goaded her.

"Well, then I guess we're just going to have to have a cook-off!"

"You're on, Colucci."

"Challenge accepted, Ortega," she countered as they arrived at their respective apartments.

"I'll text when I get up." *What am I doing?* Marisol thought to herself as she locked the door behind her. *He is so handsome, sweet, and manly. What do I have to offer? My illegal status and that at this time in a few months, I could be back in Honduras. This is no time to fantasize about what could be. He's a friend and a good one,* she reasoned as she lay on her couch. *Dear Lord, please guide my path. There is a reason why you've brought Felipe into my life. Please don't make this any more painful than it has to be.* She drifted off into a fitful sleep.

* * *

Felipe was mindlessly switching channels when his phone went off. He saw it was his mother and went back and forth with whether he should pick up and eventually answered.

"Hi, Mom."

"What did you today?"

"I went to church and then Bernie invited a group of us to eat."

"You went to church. How did that come to pass?" she asked out of genuine curiosity.

"My neighbor invited me."

"Oh, what's his name?"

"Her name is Marisol."

"Oh, well it's good to know there is una donna anziana looking after you."

"She's not an old lady. Mom, what's up?"

"Nothing. I'm not trying to start anything, I promise. But I did want to tell you that Sandra is no longer seeing the man you claimed she was going out with."

"Are you serious? If you continue talking about Sandra, I'm going to hang up," he said feeling disheartened but not surprised.

"Okay, okay. I'm sorry. It's just that it's frustrating for me to see you take an Ivy League education and waste it. Why on earth would you want to live in a crowded city when you can live in the suburbs and practice medicine in a place where you can make money?"

"This is where we're different. I'm not interested in material things. What I am interested in is making a difference. Making a difference in a place where it will matter."

Felipe heard a determined knock on the door. "Mom, I have to go, there's someone at my door."

Victoria sighed deeply. "Okay, Felipe. Please don't let too much time go by without calling me. I love you."

"Love you too, bye." He hurriedly walked toward the door

as the knocking got more persistent.

"Hey, Fatima. What's going on? Shouldn't you be gone already? Come in."

"I'm leaving in about an hour. I can't find my spare key for Marisol's apartment. I've been trying to call her, but it goes straight to voicemail," Fatima explained.

"That's not like her," he responded as he walked toward the kitchen. "She was expecting something from Amazon the other morning and she left me a copy of her key so I could leave it in her apartment before I went to work." He grabbed the key and they headed next door.

Felipe knocked first gently and then with frustration. "Colucci? Open up. It's me. Felipe." No response. As they entered, they could hear the sound of the TV, which provided temporary relief believing that since she was a sound sleeper, she had not heard them.

"Oye, Marisol. You scared us." Fatima turned on the light and it took their eyes a while to focus and take in her condition. She was laying on the couch on her back. Her cheeks were bright red and drops of perspiration lined her forehead and the top part of her hair. She was covered with a blanket.

Felipe got closer and sprang into doctor mode. He removed the blanket with urgency. "Fatima, find a thermometer and fill up the tub with cool water. Not cold. Cool." Slipping into the role of a nurse, she obliged.

He knelt on the floor, and as her temperature was registering, he was taking her sweatshirt off. The thermometer read 103.1. "Follow me to the bathroom," he barked as he carried Marisol. She was starting to wake up as he picked her up.

"Hey, Ortega, what are you doing? Are you ready to start cooking? Oh, you want to make wine? Fatima, you can help, as long as you don't sing."

"What's wrong with her?" Fatima asked.

"She's delirious. Just ignore her," he said.

Marisol looked at Felipe with disgust and started tearing up. "You told Fatima to ignore me. Hey, why are we in the bathroom?"

"Marisol," he said with authority. "Focus. You need to take your clothes off and —"

"Not with you here!" she retorted.

"Of course not. Fatima is going to help you get in the tub. Your fever is extremely high, and we have to bring it down or take you to the hospital." Knowing that she could not go to the hospital, she painfully made the effort to cooperate. "Keep her in there for a few minutes and when she dresses make sure it's something very light. I'm going to run out to the pharmacy. I'll be right back."

Fatima helped her undress and carefully helped her into the tub. She made her sit up while she poured the cool water over her extremely warm body. Goosebumps covered her, and even though she trembled, she felt comfortable. She carefully soaped her body and Fatima poured more water on her. She was about to step out of the tub when Fatima took a look at her hair.

"Oye, let's wash your hair because that ponytail looks like it's been electrocuted." She washed Marisol's hair and then helped her out of the tub wrapping a towel around her. Fatima carefully sat her down on the toilet seat. "I'm going to get some fresh PJs for you. Stay sitting. You good?"

Marisol nodded her head.

"Let me tell you something," Fatima continued as she reentered the bathroom with a fresh change of clothes. "I don't care what you say. He's into you. El médico was in a conga step when he saw how sick you are."

"He's a doctor," Marisol weakly said.

"Yes, but he's a pee-pee doctor. Which makes it easier to do all the sex with him."

"Seriously, Fatima? What would your mom say if she heard you talk like this?"

"I don't see her here. Besides, I can talk to my mom about anything," she replied. "My father's a different story," she mumbled.

"Felipe is a doctor. And doctors go into that frantic mode when they see a need. Don't you watch *Chicago Med* anymore?"

Fatima ignored Marisol as she dressed her. She brushed her hair out and added cologne as if she were fixing up a doll. She helped her to the couch and was putting socks on her when they heard the door.

"Mira, llegó el rey de Roma," Fatima said, referring to Felipe as the king of Rome.

"Shhh. You're so loud," Marisol scolded. But seeing the hurt look on her friend's face, she followed up with, "But I love you, mama."

Fatima blew her a kiss.

"Okay," he said as he sat on the couch with Marisol. He felt her forehead and shook his head no as he went back and got the thermometer. Her temperature was down to 101.2. "Still not good. I got you a prescription for an antibiotic and got some Tylenol." He gave her the first dose of both. "You need to take these around the clock."

Fatima's phone buzzed with a text. "My ride's here. Marisol, I hate to leave you like this, and my parents aren't home."

"Fatima, you go. It's not a problem because I'm staying."

Marisol's eyebrows shot up. "Hey, no one has to stay. I'm going to be fine." She stood up and turned around so quickly that she was even surprised by her sudden lack of strength.

He caught her by her elbows and helped her back down. "You were saying?"

"You work tomorrow. I can't impose on you like that," she said softly.

"Friends don't call this an imposition. You would do the same for me. Or at least I think you would," he smiled and winked.

"Of course, I would. Except for the part of writing you a prescription."

"Of course," he agreed.

Fatima watched the exchange in disbelief. *And she says there's nothing between them* she thought. "Bueno, I have to take off." She stood and waved at both of them. "I will call my mom when I get to the hotel and tell her you're not going to work tomorrow."

"I have to work tomorrow," she protested.

In unison, both Felipe and Fatima musically responded, "Noooo."

"You can't go to work tomorrow," he followed up.

"Listen to the doc. He knows what he's doing, I mean saying." She winked at Marisol, who rolled her eyes in response.

"I'm going to get some of my stuff. I'll be right back. Stay put."

"I'm not going anywhere," Marisol assured him.

She was watching reruns of *Friends* when she heard him come in. He was sporting sweatpants and a T-shirt that outlined every muscle in his body.

"Put your stuff in Doña Tomasina's old room," Marisol

directed Felipe, with neither one of them knowing that the room would soon be his.

"When did you start reading the Bible?" she asked him as she watched him make himself comfortable on the recliner.

"I told you. I grew up in church. After we got back from lunch today, I went hunting for my old Bible. When I was younger, I loved reading the book of Luke."

"Why Luke?" Before he could even respond, she acknowledged, "He was a doctor. That's cool. You know, he traveled with Paul the Apostle. That's my guy. He reminds me so much of my dad."

"Because he was a missionary, right?"

"Yeah," she whispered sadly but gained control at the same time.

"Well, you know, Luke and Paul were really good friends. Luke also went around as an investigative reporter interviewing people who were eyewitnesses of Jesus' life."

"That's right. You know, I used to talk to my dad about that. People that were there and saw Jesus was alive would have no reason to lie. I mean really. They had nothing to gain from lying. My dad used to say that the Bible is the most misunderstood book."

"Your dad was a wise man."

"He was," she said with a pensive tone. "I asked my dad once why we had to go to church if we could just pray in our house. I used to tell him that I could talk to Jesus anywhere I was."

"What did he say?"

"He told me that it was good for Christians to assemble and learn about Jesus' life and talk about him. Also, it provides a strong support system. I found that when I first got here. People that attend churches and start looking for flaws in others are missing the point of being in church. That's what I love about Iglesia de la Esperanza y Victoria. Everyone is always looking for ways to support others."

"That's the vibe I got. Bernie is an awesome person, so I always knew there had to be something worthwhile going on there." They continued to chat, and before they knew it, four hours had gone by. Her temperature was 100.2 when he brought her the next dose of Tylenol.

"Okay, your antibiotic is due at six a.m. You need to get some sleep."

"Your shift is two to ten thirty, right?"

"That's right," he nodded with a slight smile. Deep down, he liked that she knew his schedule.

"Why don't you go back to your apartment. You really don't —"

He rolled his eyes at her and shook his head no. "We settled this hours ago. I'll be fine in the spare room." He gently guided her through the French doors into her small well-kept bedroom. He moved the decorative pillows off the bed and helped her lay down.

"Wait," she said as he was leaving the bedroom. "Let's pray together."

He walked back over and sat on the side of the bed. "You pray." They took each other's hands, and he could feel that her hands were still hot from the fever.

Marisol gently started. "Heavenly Father, we thank you for this day even if it ended with me getting sick. Thank you that we both have jobs, a roof over our heads, food on the table, and all the other blessings that we might not remember now. Thank you for the people you have brought in each of our lives. Safe travels for Fatima, Rosa, and Bernie. Jesus, I pray that you will reconcile Felipe with his mom." She felt his hands stiffen at the mention of his mother. "Take care of Anthony no matter where he is, and I pray that he and I are able to find each other again. Lastly, thank you for blessing me with a friend like Felipe. Amen."

"Amen," he echoed. "Okay, get some sleep." He kissed her on the head as she rolled over onto her side. He closed the doors and took the glass to the sink. He was rinsing it out when he noticed her calendar. Her was schedule neatly written on each day with his right below. He smiled.

Right before she fell asleep, Marisol silently prayed. *Jesus, please help me with my immigration status. I know I'm running out of time. And I'm definitely out of options.*

* * *

Felipe opened his eyes as if the alarm had been going off. *Proverbs 3:5. What about Proverbs 3:5? What does it say?* These thoughts were the alarm. He sat up and looked at the time on his phone. It was 3:05 a.m. He had given Marisol her second dose about an hour before and had been relieved when he saw that her temperature was dropping. He laid back down and went back to sleep. He would look up the verse the next day.

Chapter 7

The smell of coffee roused her from a deep sleep. She sat on her bed and could hear Felipe moving around in the kitchen. She got up and still felt a little dizzy, but nowhere near as sick as the night before. She made herself presentable and headed for the kitchen.

"Good morning," she said.

"Good morning. How are you feeling? I went down to the deli while you were sleeping and bought fresh bagels."

"Ooh. They look awesome. I feel much better. Hey, you have to let me know how much I owe you."

"Owe me for what?"

"Umm. The antibiotics, Tylenol, supplies."

He started again rolling his eyes.

"Nothing. Okay, a bottle of wine. There. Don't be ridiculous."

"I don't like being presumptuous," she replied as she spread cream cheese on her bagel and looked for a reaction from him.

He sat down across from her. "Duly noted," he replied. "You

need to relax today. I mean it. Don't think because you feel better that you can resume all your activities. Give your body a chance to recover."

"I guess," she muttered.

"Rosa called me earlier to see how you are feeling."

"I'll call her later. Did you get any sleep at all?"

"Of course, I did. You don't realize that when I've worked overnight shifts and my patients are in labor, I sometimes take a nap. There's nothing much I can do until they've reached the birthing stage."

"You mean to tell me while those women are in agony, you can sleep?" she smiled.

"I told you. There's nothing else I can do. If it's difficult labor, sometimes I'll stay with them or check in more often." He did the breakfast dishes and told Marisol he would check in on her later.

* * *

She spent the rest of her day reading and resting up. She showered again around 5:30 and then heard Rosa come in while she was braiding her hair.

"Rosa, I'm in the bathroom. I'll be right out."

"Si mi hija. Take your time." Rosa helped herself to the kitchen and started to set the table for two. She methodically began to season the steaks and had started to boil the water for rice by the time Marisol joined her. Before she even had a chance to ask her what she was doing, Rosa was feeling her forehead. "Oye, you feel a little warm again."

"No, I'm down to 100, but Felipe said it's just my body fighting the flu. Once I've had a full round of antibiotics, the fever will go. He also said that when you're sick, your temperature at night will elevate a little." She noticed that Rosa was smiling. "Why are you smiling?"

"Seems like el médico is taking good care of you and I think you are, como dicen los Americanos? Smitten like a kitten."

"Ay Rosa. You and Fatima. He's just being who he is. A doctor. He would have done the same for you, Fatima, or anyone in this building. Hey, how was your conference?"

"It was good. Met a lot of new drug reps and saw a lot of the old ones."

"Change of scenery too. Oye, what are you cooking there? Smells good. And why aren't you home?" she asked as she snuck a plantain off the plate that housed the bundle Rosa had already cooked.

"Bernie is working late tonight. He was asked to cover a shift. And I was worried about you. I didn't want you to eat by yourself. Don't change the subject. We were talking about Felipe," Rosa reminded Marisol. "How much does he know?"

"Well, he knows how I got here. He also knows that unless this problem can be resolved within the next couple of months, I have to go back."

"When are you seeing the lawyer at that center you went to?"

"September 3. And he should be able to tell me something."

"Remember the scripture I gave you when you first got here?"

"I do. Proverbs 3:5. 'Trust in the Lord with all your heart; do not depend on your own understanding.'"

"That's right. And no matter what happens, you cling to that verse. Bueno, let's sit down and eat."

They sat down, unfolded their napkins, and bowed their

heads with Rosa taking the lead in prayer. "Heavenly Father, thank you for this meal and for providing for us daily. Thank you for taking care of my chiquitita. Thank you in advance for the miracle you are going to do in Marisol's life. We thank you for Bernie, Felipe, and Fatima and ask that you provide them with traveling mercies on their way home. In Jesus' name, amen." They hungrily picked up their forks and began to eat and chat, looking like a mother and daughter catching up at the end of a long day.

* * *

"Mabel, you're doing well and so is your baby. I'm going to sign your release papers and you can go home." Felipe directed himself to the husband. "Make sure she gets rest. It was a long labor." Felipe smiled at the proud new parents and went to the nurse's station to update Mabel's chart.

"Dr. Ortega," the charge nurse interrupted. "Dr. Hernandez left a note for you."

"Okay, thank you," Felipe responded without even looking up. He finished the chart and picked up the note from the desk which read: *Felipe, come and see me when you have a chance. I'm in the P 3:5.*

Felipe knew it was the Preemie unit hall 3 bed 5. But he instantly saw a second message. *Proverbs 3:5.* There it was again. And he had forgotten earlier in the day to check on that verse. He headed to the unit to meet with Dr. Hernandez and then down to the cafeteria where he ran into Bernie who was going in the same direction.

"Hey Bernie, how was New Jersey?"

"Fast. We got back and I got asked to cover a shift. Hey,

Fatima told us about Marisol."

"She's better. Low-grade temp today, but nothing like last night. I told her she shouldn't go back to work until she spends an entire day without a fever. But we both know that she's stubborn."

"Yes, she is," Bernie laughed.

Felipe felt his phone vibrate and saw he had a text from Marisol.

Going to sleep. Thank you for everything. Hope you had a good night. Going to work tomorrow. Don't be mad! Be safe walking home and don't forget to say your prayers before bed.

Good night Colucci. I'll see you soon. I could never be mad at you.

"When is the next Bible study?" Felipe asked.

"That came out of nowhere. It's Wednesday night. I've never asked you to go because we're both here. Why the sudden interest?" Bernie asked.

"Something really strange happened last night. At 3:05 a.m. I opened my eyes as if it was one in the afternoon. And when I did, in my head, I thought Proverbs 3:5. Just like that out of nowhere. Then, it happened again tonight when I was called to the Preemie Unit ward 3 bed 5. I felt it again in my spirit. Proverbs 3:5. I meant to look it up in the morning, but I was running around and forgot."

"Proverbs 3:5 is 'Trust in the Lord with all your heart and do not depend on your own understanding,'" Bernie informed him. "But first you saw it in your head and then in your spirit."

"My understanding of what?" Felipe asked, baffled.

"I've had that experience when God is trying to show me something or is going to ask me to do something. Felipe, be sensitive to the spirit of God. I know you've been away from

74

the church for a bit, but it doesn't matter. You've always been a believer and God is going to use you in mighty ways. This may have something to do with your family. And maybe not. You just have to wait and see." He paused to let Felipe absorb what he had just told him. "Well, Marisol, Rosa, and Fatima attend Wednesday Bible study. So you'll be in good company."

"Sounds good. I'll be there."

"How are you able to swing this if you work nights?"

"Dr. Menendez asked me to switch with him indefinitely."

"And it was okayed just like that?" Bernie asked.

"Yeah. Strange, huh? But I'm not complaining." Felipe finished his coffee and kept Bernie company while he ate a snack. He walked him back to the ER and then went home.

* * *

"Hola chicas!" Fatima shouted on Wednesday as she entered the discount store with Rosa and Marisol doing inventory. She greeted them each with a hug and a kiss.

"How was the conference?" Marisol asked.

"It was good. It was really good to hear actual attorneys giving presentations. And the seminar was about ethics, but they had mini-sessions that you could attend on different topics."

"Did you attend any of those?" Rosa asked.

"I did." She looked at Marisol. "I went to one on immigration law." She directed her attention back to her mom as well, "But I went to the wrong room and by the time I got to the right room, the first speaker was done. I didn't catch his name because I was so frustrated at being late that it took me a few minutes to get settled. The second one was good, but I heard the first one was awesome. He was hot too!"

Marisol giggled and Rosa shook her head with a smile knowing full well her daughter would be passing such an assessment.

"I couldn't stop looking at him, and when he smiled at me, ay Dios mio!" Fatima swooned. "I waited around to see if I could talk to him because he was looking at me. I know he was. But there were too many people waiting to speak to him and I had to go to the next presentation. Bueno, enough about me. How are you feeling?"

"I'm fine. I rested on Monday and Tuesday I woke up fine," Marisol replied.

"Mom, let me tell you something about little Miss Marisol here. You should have seen the way her mediquito was taking care of her the night she got sick. He carried her like he was el Príncipe Azul."

"Fatima, he helped me out because I was sick. He's a doctor. He would have done the same for you or your mom."

Rosa looked at Marisol with the wisdom of a mother. She knew that Marisol was starting to see Felipe differently.

"I know I feel blessed to have a handsome guardian angel as a friend," Marisol added.

"Who's a guardian angel?" asked Felipe who had caught the last part of Marisol's sentence.

"Fatima." Marisol thought quickly on her feet. "She kind of met someone at the conference that looked like an angel."

"How do you 'kind of' meet someone?" Felipe asked.

"I'll explain later," Marisol responded.

"And what brings you here, doctor?" Fatima asked.

"He's coming with us to Bible study," Marisol said.

"Oh, I see," Fatima said as she turned around to face her

mother who was smiling.

Realizing that it was later than they thought, Marisol, Rosa, Fatima, and even Felipe pitched in to get the store closed.

The mid-week service was always crowded, but people sat in their regular seats and they always knew to leave Rosa several seats. Pastor Melvin had started the service on time and was just beginning to wrap up.

"What happens when our plans don't work out? In the book of John, we learn that 'here on earth you will have many trials and sorrows' Bad things happen even when you are walking with Jesus, and sometimes we don't end up where we think we will. But remember, God can use a situation to calm your storm. He wants you to be at peace. If you haven't been in church for a while, in his letter to the Corinthian church, Paul said 'no eye has seen, no ear has heard, and no mind has imagined what God has prepared for those who love Him.'" Pastor Melvin looked straight— what seemed like to Marisol—in her direction. "We have to look at the big picture of God's promise because He. Will. Not. Fail. You. Don't put faith in faith. Put faith in God. And I will leave you with this final scripture. It's in Proverbs 3:5."

The congregation could be heard thumbing through the thin leaf-like pages looking for the final scripture of the evening. "Even when the Holy Spirit puts something in your heart that doesn't make sense to you, it's part of God's plan for you. Proverbs 3:5 gives us wisdom. 'Trust in the Lord with all your heart; do not depend on your own understanding.' Thank you for attending tonight. If you are interested in helping with the fall carnival, please don't forget to sign up at the welcome center."

The last few days of August had been unseasonably cool

in the evenings. They stood outside, each downloading the service in their way until Fatima spoke.

"Oye, I'm hungry. Marisol, you must be starving because you didn't have dinner. You too, Mom," said Fatima.

"Si, let me text Bernie to see if he can join us. Let's just go to Dunkin' Donuts since it's close."

* * *

Felipe sipped his coffee and stared at Marisol. He could see she was a million miles away.

"That was an incredible service," Fatima declared as she bit into her jelly donut.

"Yes, it was," Rosa agreed, "but we have to keep it in our hearts. Especially when things are tough. It's a risky thing to have faith, but as Pastor Melvin said, God's promises are yes and amen."

Fatima looked over at Marisol who was stirring her coffee.

"Marisol, did the dog get your tongue?"

Marisol smirked at her friend's mistake. "It's 'did the cat get your tongue'?"

"Ay, cat. Dog. Who cares? You haven't said a word since we got here."

"That's because we're listening to you," Marisol said, perking up a bit. Fatima looked over at Felipe.

"Y tu que? You haven't said much either."

"I'm just tired," he lied instead of telling her that he was replaying the service in his head. "I haven't worked days in a while—"

"I thought you worked nights," Fatima questioned.

"I do. But there is a doctor that needs to work at night, so my shift has been changed to days for a while."

Rosa's phone vibrated. "Bernie can't make it. Felipe, he told me to tell you that he'll call you tomorrow."

"Okay." Felipe nodded, picked up the check against everyone's protestations, and went to the cashier to pay.

Rosa took advantage of his absence from the table. "Marisol, what's wrong, mama. You look so sad."

"I guess I'm still wiped out from that nasty bug I had."

"Okay, ladies. Ready?" Being a gentleman, he was not about to allow three women to walk home alone.

* * *

"You really were awfully quiet tonight," Felipe said as they were walking toward their apartment doors.

"I'm just tired. The service was also really powerful."

"Yes, it was," he agreed. He could see that there was something else on her mind. "You're thinking about next Thursday, aren't you?"

She nodded with glassy eyes.

He sighed, "You know, you are such a fun person to hug," he said as he took her in his arms. There was always such a sense of peace in her presence that it broke his heart to see her worried. "Remember what we talked about tonight. God has never abandoned you. You've been through fire and come out the other end."

"I know. I have faith that everything is going to work out. Felipe?"

"Hmm?" he said, still hugging her.

"We never had that cook-off."

He smiled. *That's my girl,* he thought." Name the day and

time."

"Saturday?"

"You're on."

"I'll invite Fatima too. She loves to cook."

"As long as she doesn't sing."

Marisol laughed. She pulled back, stood on her tippy toes, and kissed him on the cheek. "Thank you, Ortega."

"No hay de que, Colucci," he said again, reassuring someone else that there was no need to thank him.

Chapter 8

I t was the last Saturday in August. The days were still warm, but the mornings and the early evenings were evidence that fall was on the horizon. Marisol and Felipe had flipped a coin the night before. Heads Italian. Tails Spanish. Tails won, so they were cooking a Spanish meal. Marisol had gotten up early and gone to the bodega to buy what she needed to make black beans. Felipe was cooking Boliche, and Fatima was making the rice and a flan. Since Marisol had a bigger kitchen, they decided to use hers and make the meal in one place.

"Okay, so I've cleared the kitchen counter, so we have space. Felipe, you can season the Boliche, and I'm going to cook the beans. Once the beans are boiling, then I'll get out of your way and you can use the stove."

Fatima stared at her. "You were up the entire night figuring this out, weren't you?"

"You know me so well." Marisol pinched Fatima's cheek.

"Bueno, and what about me? What do I do when the two of

you are doing the kitchen tango?" Fatima said.

"I was getting to that," Marisol responded.

"Of course you were," Felipe chimed in.

"Now you're learning," Fatima said to him.

"Never mind," Marisol scolded. "Okay, Fatima, your part is last. So relax, mira, play music for us."

Felipe abruptly turned to look at Marisol. "On the radio, Fatima," he said.

"I know," she said as if anything else would have been ludicrous.

Marisol was chopping an onion and a green pepper while Felipe was seasoning the meat.

They had been working for a while when she took a peek over at Felipe. "Don't you stab the meat?"

"Excuse me?" he asked with a smile.

"If you stab it, you can put condiments inside."

"Duly noted. Colucci did you —" Felipe stopped talking as he heard Fatima attempting to sing along to Steve Perry's "Sherry."

"Oooh Sherry, oh zone, oh zone," Fatima screeched out.

"And that would be," Marisol cued Felipe, "*oh, Sherrie, our love, holds on, holds on*" they sang together in a whisper while they laughed. Felipe got distracted by his phone going off.

"Hey, bro!" Alex, he mouthed to Marisol. "Like you have to ask. Remind me to hit you when I see you," he joked with his brother. "Change trains at Grand Central and take the seven or the A train uptown. Get off at 191 Street and then just walk up one block. Your timing is perfect because my friends and I are cooking a special dinner so we're setting a place for you." He paused. "No, there's no one crying here. Oh, that's Marisol's best friend singing. She's a trip. Okay. Okay, bye." He turned to Marisol, "That was Alex, and he wants to spend the week in the city to see how it would work for him work-wise."

"Oh, that's awesome!" Marisol responded. "We really have to hustle," she added as she checked the beans. "The beans are starting to get soft, but they still have a bit to go. I'm going to cover them and then you'll have more room to use the stove."

"That's perfect timing because I'm going to brown the meat. I seasoned it the way my dad does, so this is like an Ortega recipe," he said with a half-smile.

"Well, I'll have you know that my mother's black beans were famous in Honduras," she teased right back. "I'm going to do a couple of things in the apartment and then send Fatima in to start her flan."

Marisol walked into the living room to find Fatima dancing to the soundtrack from "Saturday Night Fever."

"Oye, disco queen," she teased.

"Leave me alone. I'm dancing with the hot stranger I saw at the conference."

"Bueno, when you're done, the kitchen is ready for you to start the flan. We have one more person coming for dinner."

"Who?" Fatima asked.

"Felipe's brother," Marisol responded.

"Is he hot?"

"He looks a little like Felipe. I've only seen him in pictures. Go, get your flan groove on."

Fatima scurried to the kitchen and saw that Felipe was almost finished browning the meat. "I won't get in your way," she advised him.

"No worries. There's room for both of us. Hey, Marisol told me you met some mysterious guy at the conference."

"Well, we didn't exactly meet. I was late and then I tried to see him after, but there were too many people waiting in line, and I had to go to the next presentation. But what a shame. He was soooo cute and smart."

"Are we talking about Mr. Handsome Stranger?" Marisol lovingly taunted her.

"Ay, yes we are," she said like a lovesick teenager as she placed her hand over her heart.

"Bueno, the flan is cooking. The rice we'll make a few minutes before we eat so it's fresh."

"The meat is cooking as well, and I have it on medium. I have to check it periodically, so I'm going to stick around," Felipe said.

"And," Marisol added as she checked the beans, "this has about another hour. So I say we watch a movie."

The girls settled on the couch and Felipe took his new spot, the recliner. He periodically got up to check the meat as did Marisol with the beans and Fatima with the flan. The movie was over, and the trio went into the kitchen to check their creations.

"The meat is ready," Felipe said as he shut off the burner.

"So are the beans," Marisol reported as she also turned off her burner.

"The flan came out dry," Fatima said disappointed."Pero, that's not a problem. That's when Cuban bakeries come in handy. I'll be right back." She grabbed her purse, ran down the hall, and out the door.

* * *

Fatima walked into the bakery fumbling with her purse and

phone when she reached for the counter to grab a number and realized someone else had the same idea as they bumped into each other.

"I'm so—" she started to say sorry when she fixated her eyes on the tall dark-haired stranger, who she immediately recognized as the attorney that had spoken at the conference.

God, is this you answering my prayer? You brought this beast of a man to Washington Heights just for me? His deep voice brought her back to reality.

"I'm not," he responded to the beautiful, sexy brunette standing in front of him. "I'm Alex," he extended his hand.

"I'm Fatima," she extended her hand and dropped her cell phone. She reached down to get it and bumped heads with him as he was trying to do the chivalrous thing and pick it up for her.

"I'm sorry," they said in unison and then laughed.

"You look familiar. I know that sounds like a tremendous line, but I feel like I have seen you somewhere," he responded.

"You spoke at a conference I attended recently, only I didn't get to hear you because I was late. I tried to see you after, but you had a huge crowd waiting to see you and I didn't want to be late for my next session."

Alex snapped his fingers once he made the connection."University of New Haven," he said. *If you only knew that I thought about you for days after that conference,* he thought. "Do you live around here?"

"I do. I live around the corner. I just came to pick up dessert. I'm having dinner with friends."

"Oh, I'm having dinner with my brother and his friends. What are you getting?"

"The flan here is really good," she responded.

"Excellent. Señorita, dos flanes de los grande," he said instructing the server to give him two family-size flans.

Oh my God, and he speaks Spanish. Can he hear my heart beating? Okay, Fatima, you've got this. Give him some money for the flan. Now," she scolded herself.

He noticed that she was going for her wallet. "You're not giving me anything for this. I took your ticket, accidentally of course." He smiled, and it reminded her of someone, but she couldn't remember who.

"Are you sure?" she asked.

"Positive. You can help me get to my brother's apartment. It's the first time I've been to this part of the city."

"Si como no. I'll help you get there."

And she speaks Spanish, he thought.

He opened the door to the bakery for her to walk through and he was taken by her beauty and her endearing kooky personality. They had been walking for a couple of minutes and chatting when Fatima realized they were heading for the same building. *Wait a second. He's having dinner with his brother and friends. It couldn't be.*

"Are you headed for 460?" she asked.

"Yes, why?" he replied.

"Are you Felipe's brother?" she continued the minor inter-rogation.

"Yes, do you know him?"

"He's my neighbor, and he works with my dad!" *Already a connection. I love it.*

"Okay, so now I know two people in the building. I'm staying with my brother for a week because I work in the city and I'm going to be relocating soon."

Fatima felt her heart do the cha cha cha at hearing this news.

"Oh, that's good," she replied trying to sound aloof.

* * *

Marisol and Felipe had cleaned up the kitchen and were starting to transfer the food to serving dishes so they could wash the pots. He noticed that she was putting a small portion in the blender.

"Why are those in the blender?" he asked.

"Oh, because I like to eat them like a puree, so I always do a small portion for myself." She turned the blender on for five seconds, then stopped it to stir the concoction and make sure every bean was pureed. Turned it back on. Nothing. "Why is this thing not turning back on?"

She went to make sure the plug was all the way in when she noticed a few beans were stuck to the side. She stuck a spoon inside the blender and was stirring when Felipe noticed the problem.

"Oh, it's the circuit breaker," he said as he hit it, not realizing Marisol still had a spoon in the blender. He watched in shock as the blender erupted like a volcano and all over Marisol.

"Are you okay?" he asked, knowing that she was except for the fact that she was wearing the beans. He was trying desperately not to laugh.

The thick mixture coated her eyelashes like someone who has put on too much mascara. Her smooth skin was covered, and she had streaks of black in her hair. "And you're laughing," she said trying to suppress a smile herself.

"I'm not. I'm really sorry. I didn't see that the spoon was still in there," he said, although the more he denied it, the harder he laughed. He pulled out a rogue bean from her curls as he tried to compose himself.

"It's okay. Laugh," she said as she wiped her eyes and face. "I bet you won't think it's funny if we hugged now, right?"

He instantly lost his grin. "You wouldn't."

"Wouldn't I?" She started to chase him around the apartment. They ended up back in the kitchen where he gave in for no other reason than to steal a hug. They were both laughing hysterically until they realized that Alex and Fatima were standing in the kitchen as well.

"What happened here?" Alex asked with a smirk.

"Do you see why these two can't be left alone?" Fatima responded.

Felipe walked toward his brother with his arms open as if to hug him.

"Don't you dare," Alex said with a smile.

"Alex, this is Marisol. Marisol, Alex."

"I'll shake your hand later," she laughed.

"Don't worry. Felipe's told me a lot about you," he said.

"All good, I hope," she said with a smile. "I'm going to take a shower after I clean this up."

"No," Fatima interjected, "you go take a shower and I'll clean up"

"I'll help you," Alex added as he was rolling up his sleeves.

"Where's your bag, Alex? I'll take it to my place," Felipe offered.

"It's by the door," he responded as he was helping Fatima pick up pieces of the blender top.

* * *

Twenty minutes later, Felipe came back dressed in khaki pants and a black shirt. Fatima and Alex had finished cleaning up the kitchen and were sitting in the living room talking as if they had known each other for years.

"Where's Marisol?" Felipe asked as he gave his brother a welcoming hug.

"She's still getting ready," Fatima replied.

"Alex, we're going to set up the table in the living room so we have more room. Come help me move it, and there's another one in the wine room we have to bring out here."

Marisol came out in her white shorts, black top, and her hair neatly done in a French braid.

"Hi Alex," she greeted him with a handshake and kiss on the cheek. "I'm more presentable now to say hello," she smiled.

"No worries, it's nice to meet you," he reciprocated her warmth.

Felipe and Alex left to get the table from Felipe's apartment, leaving Marisol and Fatima relaxing on the couch. Marisol got up to make sure they had left before interrogating Fatima.

"Okay, spill. How did the two of you end up here together?" she smiled.

"I still can't believe it. That's the attorney that was at the seminar I attended!"

"Noooo."

"Yeees! He was at the bakery picking up dessert and we both went for the same serving number. So he ended up getting both desserts and I told him I would help him get to his brother's house. But as we were approaching the building, I put two and two together."

"That is crazy!"

"I know!!! Just as crazy as the black beans wrapped around you and Felipe. And don't think I missed that hug. What happened?"

Marisol filled her in on the black bean caper.

* * *

"Let me know if you need more room," Felipe told his brother who was putting his stuff away in the closet. "So what did you think of her?"

"Fatima? She's beautiful and funny."

"Not Fatima. Marisol."

"I've known her for five minutes. But she seems really nice. You look different than the last time I saw you."

"How?"

"You look relaxed. Happy."

"Happy, yes. Relaxed, definitely after this coming Thursday."

"What's this Thursday?"

"I'll tell you about it later. Let's get this table over to Marisol's."

* * *

The Gonzalezes arrived half an hour later and after introductions were made and some small talk had taken place, they sat down for dinner. After they said grace, they dug in.

"Felipe made the meat, I made the beans, and Fatima the rice," Marisol announced.

"Fatima made a flan that ended up looking like a cardboard box," Fatima said about herself.

"Ahh," Alex interrupted, "but, if Fatima had not done that, I wouldn't have run into her at the bakery and would probably still be walking around Washington Heights looking for my brother's building," he said as he winked at her.

Fatima kicked Marisol under the table to get her to notice the special compliment Alex had just paid her.

"Ouch. Fatima, why did you kick me?" Marisol said rubbing her shin.

"Was that your leg? Ay, I'm sorry," Fatima replied, widening her eyes.

"What kind of wine is this? It's really good," Alex said.

"Marisol made it," Felipe proudly responded.

"Actually, Felipe and Fatima helped me a lot," Marisol humbly admitted.

"It's very good," Bernie and Rosa agreed.

* * *

"Are you ready for Thursday?' Rosa gently asked Marisol as they were putting the dishes away.

"I am."

"What time is your appointment?"

"Four."

"Do you want me to go with you?"

"No, I'll be fine."

"Why don't you take Felipe or Fatima with you?"

"No, really. I'll be fine. Please don't worry."

"I'm not. I have faith that you're going to be just fine."

"Me too," Marisol said as she hugged Rosa.

Chapter 9

The four days leading to Thursday flew by. Felipe, Alex, and Fatima were working, and Marisol had taken the afternoon off to take care of some errands before her appointment.

How are you holding up? Felipe texted her around three p.m.

I'm good. Looking forward to this appointment because I feel like something is getting done.

Text me as soon as you get out. We'll go get something to eat.

Sounds good.

Before he put his phone away, he texted his brother.

What time do you get out?

In five minutes. Why?

I need to talk to you about something. I'll see you at home.

Okay.

* * *

Alex was easily adjusting to how simple it was to live and work in the same city. The office was thirty minutes away from the apartment and it was a straight shot on the express. Felipe had told Alex Marisol's story one night and he had volunteered his services if things didn't go well with the lawyer Marisol had hired. He had also been spending more time with Fatima and getting to know her. He had just gotten home and was relaxing on the couch when he heard Felipe come in.

"Hey, you sounded serious. I know today is Marisol's appointment. Have you heard anything?" Alex asked.

"No, she should be there now as we speak. I just have a bad feeling about this. She went there one time. The guy called her once and just told her what documents to bring. But then he never called again. I know we've talked about this on and off, but I want to solidify a plan of what the options are in case this goes south. I'm gonna take a quick shower. I'll be right out."

True to his word, Felipe was sitting with his brother fifteen minutes later.

"Okay, based on what you've told me, she has the documents to get her paperwork started. The problem is that because she didn't technically cross the border even though she has a passport that says she did if she's caught, it's fraud. She will automatically be deported," Alex explained.

"How would they be able to catch her? There's no way they would be able to track that," Felipe stated.

"You're right. It would be almost impossible. But almost is not good enough. She'd be taking a risk. There is one other way that could solidify her path to citizenship and status change. She would have to marry a United States citizen. That's a gamble too because people who get married that way run the risk of getting caught and deported."

"Unless they can pull it off," Felipe said as he locked eyes with his brother.

"That's right. Unless they can pull it off." He saw the determined look in his brother's eyes. "You can't be serious."

"But I am. Marisol has no one. Bernie and Rosa can't do anything because as much as they love her like a daughter, she's not related to them. She gets sent back to Honduras and we're basically sending her to her death." What Alex didn't know is that Felipe was one step ahead. Right before he had come home from work, he had stopped off at Joyeria Pepe and bought a single engagement ring.

"You're talking about a serious commitment. You told me she would never accept financial help from you. What makes you think she'll accept your proposal?"

"Two reasons," he responded as he held up two fingers. "The first and most important one is that she is out of options. The second one is that she knows that Mom is not going to give me the property nona left me unless I'm married. I don't care about the property, but I will use it as leverage to convince her."

"Look, you know that I'm going to support you no matter what you decide. But are you sure you want to give up at least a year and a half of your life?"

"I'm positive."

"You sure you're not falling in love with this girl?"

"We've become really good friends. I care for her, but romantic love? I don't think so."

"You should see yourself when you're around her. But if you say you're good friends, then you're just good friends." Alex thought about what he said and added, "Yeah, no. I say you love her but don't know. "He realized Felipe wasn't listening. "Hello?"

"I heard you. Love your friends."

Alex rolled his eyes and patted his brother on the back. "That's right, bro. Love your friends."

"What's going on with Fatima anyway?" he smiled.

"I like her a lot. Don't let her ditzy personality fool you. She's smart as a whip as she proved the other night quoting supreme court cases I didn't even know existed."

"I'm glad. Maybe this weekend —" Felipe felt his phone vibrate and saw it was a text from Marisol.

Please come quickly if you can.

I'm on my way.

"This can't be good," Felipe muttered under his breath.

"What's wrong?"

"I'll see you later. I'll call you," he said as he quickly went into his room to retrieve a small box. He grabbed his keys and went out the door.

* * *

Felipe could see Marisol half a block away. She was sitting on a bus bench clutching the envelope with her papers.

"What's wrong?" he asked as he sat next to her.

"Take a look inside the office."

Felipe got up and cupped his hands around his face so he could look inside. The place was completely empty and a "for rent" sign was posted on the door. He walked back to the bench and sat down again.

"Did you call? Maybe they moved."

"The number on his card has been disconnected," she said

numbly. "You know how I feel right now? Like I just had to jump off another truck," she said as she started to cry softly. "I have faith. I do. But before you got here, I was telling God that I really don't know what to do next."

He put his arm around her, and she just cried in his arms. "Marisol," he gently called her name, "look at me," he said as he lifted her chin to his face. "There's something I want to talk to you about, but not here. Let's go to La Nueva España for dinner."

Felipe had called when they were on their way and a table for two was waiting when they arrived. He waited for her to go to the restroom to wash up before he called his brother.

"Hey, we're out to dinner."

"How did it go? Is she okay?"

"I'll tell you everything later. Go to my nightstand. There's an envelope in there with money and a card from Joyeria Pepe. Go and buy two simple wedding bands. Take one of my rings and get Fatima to help you with Marisol's ring size. Okay, I have to go. She's coming back."

They walked to the restaurant silently. She smiled wanly as she approached the table and Felipe was pushing out her chair so she could sit.

"I talked to my brother today about this situation. I just wanted to be prepared with a backup plan in case we needed it. You have to promise me you're going to listen to everything I have to say before you respond."

"Okay," she nodded in agreement.

"Alex told me that the possibility existed that if your documents were found to be fraudulent, it would be grounds for deportation."

"I know."

"But there is one thing that we could do that would make a difference and solidify your application more." He took a deep breath and sighed, "I think we should get married."

Marisol looked at him puzzled. "What?"

"You said you wouldn't interrupt," he reminded her. "If we get married, it will change the trajectory of your status. There are some very specific things we would have to do, but we'll work out the details. You can talk now."

"I think it's so sweet of you to make this offer, but what about you? What would this do to your life?"

"I was prepared for you to bring that up. You remember that whole thing about my mother not giving me the property I inherited until I get married. Well, you would be helping me that way."

Marisol could see right through his noble gesture. She knew that he didn't care about that property. "It's a good thing you're a doctor because you'd make a lousy lawyer."

He smiled. "I'm totally serious and I mean every word of my offer."

"Felipe, this would benefit me. But this is too huge a sacrifice for you to make."

"At one of the services we attended, Pastor Melvin said that one decision could change the trajectory of your entire life. Do you think I could live with myself if you got deported when I could have done something? I couldn't," he paused to let her digest what he was saying. "I prayed about this," he continued, "and Proverbs 3:5 has been chasing me for the past three weeks."

Trust in the Lord and lean not on your own understanding, Marisol thought.

"And that quiet, still voice that you have described to me

time and again has been God putting it in my heart to take this step," he added. "Let's go over the particulars. If you say yes, I will move into your apartment and take the spare room. My brother wants to move to the city, so he can take my apartment. You'll have to change your last name, and as soon as we're married, I'll put you on my insurance."

"You've really thought about all the details," *except for one.* She was thinking about how to broach the subject of what his sex life would look like.

"What about, umm—"

He liked that she was talking like it was a consideration or a done deal.

"Umm, what if you want to…" she paused.

"Sex?" he asked, trying to suppress a smile. It was as if he had read her mind. "I never said we had to sleep together," he whispered.

"Yes, but maybe you want to date someone —"

"Out of the question. Neither one of us can or else we're wasting our time. We have to make this look real. And when we're out in public, we have to amp it up."

Marisol sighed. She was quiet as she considered his offer. Her only other option was to risk going back to Honduras. And then what? She had nothing to lose.

"Okay. If we do this, you need a prenuptial agreement and —"

"No way. That would arouse suspicion of a fake marriage. If I thought for one minute that you were that kind of person, we would not be having this conversation. We split all the expenses of the apartment and I'll take light and groceries."

"You know those are the only expenses I have!"

"No, you have your phone and wine-making stuff. Besides,

save your money."

"This could take up to a year and a half. You know that, right?"

"I know that."

"Here's the timeline. We'll get married tomorrow. Since we're doing it at the courthouse, they will waive the 24-hour waiting period."

"What about your family? Bernie, Rosa, and Fatima…" she sighed with apprehension.

"My brother knows of course, and he'll want to tell Fatima. Besides, it will look better if we bring our own witnesses. My family, Rosa, and Bernie will know after."

"You think of everything, don't you?"

"I try. So what do you say?"

"I don't want to go back to Honduras."

"Okay, so you'll marry me?"

"Yes."

"Okay, don't freak with what I'm about to do. We want people to see this." Removing the small box from his jacket, he got down on one knee.

Marisol's eyes widened with a half-smile as her heart raced.

"Marisol Colucci, will you marry me?"

Overcome with emotion and teary eyes at the sacrifice he was about to make for her, she whispered, "Yes." He placed the ring on her finger and kissed her cheek. A few onlookers clapped as he winked at her.

They ordered dinner and the restaurant gave them a complimentary bottle of champagne since they were regulars celebrating a special occasion. They chitchatted about trivial things as a means of taking a break from the lengthy battle they had ahead of them. On the way home, Felipe called and gave his brother the update.

* * *

When they got back to Marisol's apartment, Alex and Fatima were watching television.

"We're back," Marisol announced. She looked at Fatima. "You told me that the lawyer was suspicious and—"

Fatima stood up and just hugged Marisol. "Forget it. Just forget it. What's important now is keeping you here." Fatima had tears streaming down her face as did Marisol. They sat on the couch to compose themselves. Felipe took his place on the recliner but sat with his body arched forward as if he was in a huddle with this team.

"Okay, here's the plan for tomorrow. Let's get to the courthouse early."

"I already put in a phone call to Judge Benson. We're all set," Alex said.

"As soon as Alex called me, I called my mom and told her that the attorney had to postpone your appointment," Fatima added.

"We're going to tell them tomorrow. After the fact. So after we get married, I'm going to take Marisol to lunch. When we get back, I'll start moving my stuff in here, and you can start getting settled in my apartment."

"Oye, pero you think of everything," Fatima said with a smile when she noticed the ring on Marisol's hand. "We got the wedding bands you told us to get," she added.

"Did I give you enough or do I owe you money?" he asked his brother.

"No, we're good."

Chapter 9

"Bueno, I'm going home. We have a long day tomorrow so get some rest," Felipe advised the group. He kissed Marisol on the cheek and waited for Alex to say goodbye to Fatima, who had decided to spend the night to help Marisol get ready.

* * *

"At this time tomorrow, you will be Marisol Ortega," Fatima whispered as they lay in bed staring at the ceiling.

"I know. It's crazy."

"You know," Fatima said as she rolled to her side and propped up her elbow to support her head with her hand, "I think he's really in love with you."

Marisol looked at her shocked and rolled over as well, "No way! He's just making this sacrifice to keep me here."

"I think there's more to it than that."

"We've only known each other a little over a month."

"So? And I think you love him too." She turned over on her side again and fluffed up her pillow.

"You're too much," Marisol responded as she rolled over as well."Good night."

"Good night," Fatima sleepily responded.

"Fatima?"

"Que?" she was almost asleep.

"Thank you. I love you."

"You're welcome. I love you too."

Chapter 10

"One last time, are you sure you want to do this?" Alex asked as he was fixing Felipe's tie.

"I'm positive for the tenth time."

"I'm not trying to doubt your decision, but I just want to make sure that you really want to go through with this."

"I've never been surer of anything in a long time. I wish I could explain it, but it's almost like a conviction that this is what I need to do. It's very simple."

"I still say that you both see each other as more than just friends." He saw Felipe shaking his head no, "But that's just my observation," Alex added.

"We're just good friends," Felipe insisted.

"Okay. If you say so."

* * *

In the apartment next door, Fatima was ironing Marisol's dress. She saw her come out of the shower and go for her hair ties. "Oye, don't French braid your hair because you're getting married. You're not going to the flea market."

"I know," she replied as she was brushing out her wet hair.

"I will blow dry your hair. Start doing your makeup."

Marisol put on a light eyeshadow that brought out the color of her eyes. A little rouge and a matte lipstick that gave her a natural look. Fatima dried Marisol's hair and then instructed her to get dressed. It was the last time she could wear her white cotton summer dress that she had bought with her first paycheck. She had put it on layaway and had felt so proud the day she was able to bring it home. Her chestnut curls fell on her shoulders and her light freckles made her look as innocent as she truly was for many things, although she was good at putting up a strong front.

Are you ready? Felipe texted her.

Yes, we are. On our way out.

"Okay, this is it," Marisol said.

"You look beautiful. Let me take your picture."

They took pictures of each other and a couple of selfies together.

* * *

Felipe and Alex were downstairs already. When Marisol saw him, she was captivated by how handsome he looked. He was wearing a navy blue dark suit with a white shirt and black tie. His jet-black hair combed back, he looked to her like the cover of a GQ magazine.

This is your friend. Your friend, Felipe, who is about to make a huge sacrifice for you. But I can still acknowledge that he's hot. He is my hot friend Felipe who is about to make a commitment to be my husband, Marisol told herself not realizing that she was nodding her head.

"Why are you nodding your head?" he asked her as he kissed her lightly on the cheek.

"Was I nodding? Hmm. I was just doing a checklist in my head," she pointed at her head for emphasis, "to make sure I have everything I need."

"You look beautiful."

"Well, thank you. You look very handsome too."

"You look quite stunning yourself," Alex said to Fatima.

"And you clean up well too," she teased right back.

They took a few pictures and then headed down the block to catch the subway.

* * *

The train station was busy with people hustling to get to work. They took the subway to Franklin Street Station and then a short walk brought them to the courthouse. Marisol had never been to this side of town because there was no need. Her entire five-month existence in the States had revolved around security and safety. Church, work, Rosa, Bernie, and of course Fatima. Her small social circle was in a half-mile radius.

The big, white building was impressive to her. This is where judicial processes took place, and she had always been fascinated by the law. Just as Alex had promised, Judge Angela Benson had provided the waiver. Before they knew it, they were filling out the forms and presenting documentation. "Okay, everything looks in order," the clerk reassured them. "Judge Angela Benson will conduct the ceremony. You can have a seat while you wait."

Alex and Fatima were engaged in conversation as Marisol motioned for Felipe to bend down so she could whisper something in his ear.

"This is it. Are you sure?" Marisol asked.

"Well," he teasingly started, "yes, I am sure. I am positively sure."

A few minutes later, they were escorted into a court-room."Okay, Ms. Colucci and Mr. Ortega," Judge Benson read from the application, "are we ready?"

She had them take each other's hands. Marisol gave Fatima a small bouquet that they had bought at the subway station. After reading the beginning part of the ceremony, they exchanged vows. The witnesses served their purpose, and before they knew it, Judge Benson was ending the ceremony.

"By the powers vested in me by the state of New York, I now pronounce you man and wife. Dr. Ortega, you may kiss your bride."

He brought her closer to him and, staring right into her eyes, he gently kissed her. *Why does she look different to me now?* he thought to himself. *She's my buddy. My best friend. The one I can talk to without filtering myself. Okay, she's my gorgeous-looking buddy. I'm getting caught up in this, but that's good. We have to make it look real. But it is real. Maybe not. Okay, Ortega, you've got this.*

"Congratulations!" they simultaneously cheered breaking Felipe's trance. The newlyweds and Alex and Fatima thanked the judge and left the courthouse. Alex hugged his new sister-in-law and welcomed her to the family, and Fatima hugged Felipe. The Ortegas were on their way to start their lives as a happily married couple, even if it was a temporary act. Or so they thought. A temporary act.

"Okay, Mrs. Ortega. Where do you want to go for lunch?" Felipe asked as he watched Alex whispering in Fatima's ear as she laughed.

"I'm so hungry that anywhere is fine with me," she motioned with eyes to Fatima and Alex, and without missing a beat, Felipe picked up on what she was saying.

He looked over in his brother's direction and whistled to get his attention. "Oye, Romeo, change in plans. Why don't you and Fatima come have lunch with us? Like a little reception."

Alex looked at Fatima, who nodded yes. "Okay, where to?" he asked.

"Let's go to Havana's on 46th Street," Felipe suggested." They have awesome Cuban food."

They took the train and were in Times Square before they knew it. Marisol's eyes were wide with excitement. Looking at each billboard and the crowds in this part of the city was new to her. And she took it all in.

* * *

They arrived at the restaurant, and Fatima, who had been conspiring with Alex on the train, cornered the hostess with very specific instructions.

"Una mesa para cuatro, por favor," Felipe said, requesting a table for four.

They were seated and given the menu. Before they could order even water, a bottle of champagne was brought to the table.

"This is from Fatima and me," Alex quickly clarified.

"Oh, and we have other surprises coming too," Fatima

quickly added.

Throughout the entire meal, Felipe and Marisol couldn't take their eyes off each other and chalked it up to being caught up in the moment. They had ordered dessert when Fatima made an announcement.

"Bueno," she started as she picked up her glass of wine. "Every couple has the first dance. Even though this is not a 'formal reception,'" she used air quotes for emphasis, "I asked the restaurant to play something for the two of you to dance to. For appearance's sake, of course," she added sarcastically.

"Would Dr. And Mrs. Ortega please come to the dance floor?" a voice echoed in the restaurant.

Felipe and Marisol headed for the dance floor. He gently took her in his arms as "Hero" by Enrique Iglesias began to play. *"Let me be your hero,"* the singer whispered at the beginning of the song as Felipe felt that sentiment. He held her close and teared up with "I *can be your hero baby, I can kiss away the pain, I will stand by you forever, you can take my breath away."*

The song had ended, and they were still swaying back and forth until they heard the restaurant erupt in applause. Marisol smiled. Felipe winked at his wife and made her knees go weak. They headed back to the table where there was a small cake with a bride and groom at the top.

"How were you able to do this?" Marisol asked Fatima when they got back to their table.

"I make things happen," said Fatima.

"Yes, she does," Alex agreed.

They ate cake, took pictures, and enjoyed the rest of the afternoon. It was close to four when they headed back to Washington Heights and back to real life. Standing in front of the building, they plotted the first step, which was to tell

Bernie and Rosa.

"I texted my mom and told her to come over at about eight p.m.," said Fatima.

"Okay, we'll get some stuff to snack on," Marisol responded.

"No, you and Felipe go rest. Fatima and I will take care of that," Alex countered.

Alex and Fatima turned around and headed right back to the local bakery on St. Nicholas Avenue.

* * *

"Shall we?" Felipe asked Marisol as he held the door to the building open.

Marisol opened the door to the apartment and was about to step inside when Felipe put his arm around her and pulled her back.

"Aren't we going inside?" she asked.

"Yes, but first I want to do this." He carried her through the front door swiftly as if it was the most natural thing. She smiled at his attention to tradition. He carried her all the way down the hall and into the living room, where he gently put her down.

"I want to set things up nicely for Bernie and Rosa. I feel so bad that we excluded them," Marisol said regretfully.

"We had to do it this way," he said gently.

"I know," she said in a whisper.

Felipe sat in the living room watching the news while Marisol was setting the makeshift table they had created by again adjoining two tables together. She went into Tomasina's closet which is where she had neatly placed her kitchen linens after her passing. She chose brown placemats that had a creamsicle soft design indicative of the fall season. She picked up the matching cloth napkins, which gave off a Downy scent. She closed her eyes and thought about her friend. How kind Tomasina had been to her. She had encouraged her constantly and told her that everything would work out.

"You okay?" Felipe's voice broke through her thoughts.

"Yeah, I was just getting the stuff I need to set the table. Can you get that box from the top shelf? Tomasina's nice plate set is up there."

"Wow." He reached out over her to get the box. "You're really going all out."

"Well, it's not every day you get married."

"True," he agreed.

She set the table and joined Felipe in the living room. "So what are we going to say?"

"Simple. We've been spending a lot of time together and realized that we love each other and got married. The less we say, the better." He reached over and softly brushed one of her curls away from her eyes.

They heard Fatima and Alex coming into the apartment and stood to help them.

"Oye, did you guys think you were feeding an army?" Felipe joked.

"Mi hijo, the more food we have, the smoother the shock will be," Fatima replied out of breath. "Okay, they will be here in fifteen minutes. What's the plan?"

As soon as Felipe had filled in his accomplices, there was a knock on the door. The four of them froze and smiled.

* * *

"Bueno, what's going on?" Rosa began after they had exchanged greetings and settled themselves in the living room.

Felipe took Marisol's hand. "Marisol and I got married today." Dead air. Fatima turned to face her parents in the fashion of a reporter as if to gauge their expressions.

Rosa turned to Marisol and asked, "Why didn't you tell us anything? You said you always said you wanted to get married in the church."

"Because we wanted to elope and surprise everyone," Marisol promptly responded.

"We've become close and came to the realization that we belong together. Right, babe?" Felipe added.

"Yep." Marisol went and sat on his lap.

With knit eyebrows and mouth gaping, Fatima was looking at them as if they were posing for the cover of Good Housekeeping.

"It's just so sudden," Rosa continued. She was no dummy and she knew there was something else. She would speak to Marisol alone later.

"Bueno gente, let's eat. Me and Alex bought a ton of sandwiches," Fatima said as she got up to bring in the food.

They all ate and just filled Bernie and Rosa in on the details of the ceremony and the celebratory lunch.

* * *

"Marisol, did this have anything to do with your situation? You know that if you're found out, you will be deported," Rosa asked when the guys had gone out to play handball.

"Of course not! I love him. And he loves me. We would never put ourselves in a bad position." *Why does it feel like we're not*

110

being truthful? Oh, because we're not. We're really good friends, but not lovers. Other than the sex part, was there a difference? Focus, Marisol. Get through this conversation and you can think later.

"Where did you go?" Rosa asked her as she tried to pull her away from her thoughts.

"It's been a long day."

"Did you pray about this decision?"

And wasn't it funny she should ask. Not only had she prayed, but her petition had been answered. Just not in the way she thought.

"I did. More than you know," she said reflectively.

"Well, then there's only one thing left to say. Congratulations!" Rosa hugged her, and Fatima, not to be outdone, joined the duo.

* * *

"Aren't you going to grill me?" Felipe asked Bernie as soon as they left the building.

"No, why would I?"

"You don't seem to be as surprised as Rosa."

"I'm not. I've been watching the two of you for two months."

"Yeah, and what do you see?"

"Two people that weren't looking and found each other."

"We were neighbors and became close friends. I mean, I can tell her anything without filtering myself. You know what I mean?"

"I know exactly what you mean." *He's clueless. How can he not see it?* Bernie thought. Not wanting to make Alex feel uncomfortable, Bernie changed the subject, and the men

111

played a competitive game of handball.

"Hey," Fatima called out through the kitchen window, "we're ready for dessert."

* * *

"It's beautiful," Marisol said about the second cake that Alex and Fatima had bought.

"Not as beautiful as you," Felipe responded as he gave her that look that made her stomach jump.

He's acting. Remember, he's acting. Make memories that others will remember also. Holy cow, he's so convincing, Marisol thought. "Aww. You're too sweet. I have something too." She went to the back closet and picked up a bottle of wine she had made four months before. "This is a dessert wine."

"Oye, you have to feed each other cake," Fatima teased. Rosa picked up her phone and took pictures as both their hands sliced the first piece. With a fiendish look on her face and her heart racing, Marisol fed Felipe a spoonful and then he reciprocated. She poured the wine and the five toasted to Felipe and Marisol.

"Bueno, Bernardo," Rosa announced.

"Oh boy, when she calls me Bernardo, I know it's time to go. When are you going to see your parents to tell them?"

"Tomorrow," Felipe sighed. He hated leaving Marisol on their first day married, but it was a conversation he wanted to get over with as quickly as possible. "After church Sunday I just want to wind down because I start working Monday again and I'm back to the three to eleven p.m. shift"

"I will be back Monday, Rosa."

"Of course, Mrs. Ortega. I will see you Sunday anyway."

112

"I love the way that sounds," Fatima gushed as she got her keys out.

* * *

With the company gone and the kitchen cleaned up, they settled in the living room to debrief the day and their future.

"I'm going to see my parents early tomorrow because I want to be back early."

"You don't have to rush on my account. I have some stuff to do around here, and I want to make some more room in the closet that's in the spare room and the bathroom. How are you feeling about seeing your parents tomorrow?"

He shook his head, "I don't know. But it doesn't make a difference to me what they think."

"Well, just text me and let me know if I need to disappear," she joked.

"Nah. Don't worry. We're a force to be reckoned with now. Besides, I have the word of God. And for the past two months, it's been my weapon."

"Heaven and earth will disappear, but my words will never disappear," Marisol automatically said.

"Matthew 24:35," Felipe said.

"Very good, doctor!"

"See, I've been studying the scriptures."

"I see that. Okay, I'm going to go take a shower"

"Okay. He grabbed the remote and laid on the couch as she disappeared into the bedroom and then the bathroom. *Hey God, are you busy? I need to know what is so different and why she looks so beautiful to me now. I always thought she was cute, but it's just so different now. Why? I dated Sandra for years, and I*

113

don't think I ever felt about her the way I feel about my wife. Uh, did you just hear me? My wife. If this is an arrangement, why am I so glad I married her? I know it was the right thing to do. I feel it. But it doesn't feel like a sacrifice. Is this part of that whole thing of being a doctor and wanting to save everyone? That's probably it. Okay, I feel better.

"What in the world are you thinking about staring at the screen like that?" Marisol questioned standing in front of him wearing light pink pajama bottoms and a tank top. Her hair clipped up in a bun and the little trace of makeup she wore gone.

"I was just thinking about work," he bluffed as he looked at her from top to bottom. "That's what you had on the day we met."

She looked at what she was wearing and realized he was right. "Oh, yes, it is." *He noticed! He noticed! Check me out like a fifteen-year-old. I really need to stop. Just stop, Marisol. Why should I though?* she argued with herself.

Before she could say anything else, he was going into his bedroom with Marisol following.

"I put a towel on your bed. Tomasina's hamper was kept in the bathroom, and by the way, I call laundry. It relaxes me." *I just volunteered to wash his underwear. Okay, I have a brother. I can live with that.*

"I won't even argue because I hate laundry."

"Good. I also like to iron. So that's mine too."

He gave her the thumbs up. He set his alarm and went to take a shower. She went to the kitchen and made herself a cup of tea, and by the time she was back in her room, she could hear him in his room putting his stuff away.

"Well, I guess this is good night," she said.

"Yeah, we should go to bed," he casually responded as her eyes widened. "You know what I meant," he clarified.

Yeah, I know what you meant, she thought, a part of her disappointed. He kissed her on the cheek. "Wait," she said as she grabbed his hand, "let's pray. Heavenly Father, thank you for this day. Keep us safe and in your care with your sovereign hand over our lives. Give Felipe the words to say tomorrow as he talks to his family and never let us forget to pray about every decision we make. In Jesus' name."

"Amen," they said jointly.

* * *

In the building across the street, Bernie and Rosa were also getting ready for bed.

"You haven't said much since we left the Ortega's," Bernie said.

Rosa smiled at her husband's reference to Marisol and Felipe. "There's not much to say. I'm scared for both of them. They have a huge battle ahead with interviews and basically trying to prove that their marriage is legitimate. I don't want to see Marisol get deported or Felipe lose his career. This is an awful lie."

"Oh, they're lying all right," Bernie replied.

"I know they are," Rosa said with emphasis.

"But not in the way you think. They're not even lying to each other. They're lying to themselves. Haven't you seen the way they look at each other? Can you honestly tell me that there isn't something more? He never talked about Sandra the way he talks about Marisol. And you just have to take one look at how Marisol looks at Felipe and you know where she stands."

"You think so?"

"I know so. Mi vida, God would have never, ever allowed this to happen unless he had a plan. And I'm telling you that those two are going to be married for the rest of their lives. They just don't know it yet," he chuckled.

"But Bernie, after only one month?"

"Rosa Alvarez Gonzalez. You and I had known each other for six weeks, and if I'm not mistaken, we're going on forty years of marriage."

"Yes, we are," she responded as she looked at him the way she did when they were first married."

"Buenas Noches, princesa," he told the love of his life as he pulled the covers over himself.

"Buenas Noches, mi rey," she reciprocated as she shut her light off and kissed the man she still looked at as the love of her life.

Chapter 11

The train ride to Connecticut was uneventful, and he had rehearsed in his mind what he was going to say. The leaves were changing, and the orange and brown were beginning to dominate the landscape. *God, please give me the words to say*, he prayed as the Uber pulled up in front of his parents' house. He used his key to let himself in.

"Hello?" he called out.

"We're in the family room" Felipe Sr. called out.

He hugged and kissed his parents before he made himself comfortable on the couch.

How are things in Manhattan?" his father asked.

"Good, Dad. They're really good. You know, delivering babies and just living life."

"Alex seems to like the city. Who is Fatima?" his mother asked.

"He's doing great, Mom, and we'll talk about Fatima later," Felipe responded.

"Oh, before I forget. Sandra got married two weeks ago.

You didn't come back to tell us you want her back, did you?"

Felipe stared at his mother in total disbelief.

"No, that's not why I'm here, although I'm glad she moved on. That makes what I'm going to tell you a lot easier. I married Marisol Colucci yesterday."

"Your neighbor?" his mother asked incredulously. "Is she pregnant?"

"No, Mom. She's not pregnant. I'm in love with her."

"You've known her for about a month. How could you be in love with her?"

"She's everything I've ever wanted in a woman." And he wasn't lying when he said it. Marisol was everything Sandra was not. Loving. Humble. Beautiful and transparent. Everything he knew his mother wanted to be.

"I just don't know what kind of future you could have with a girl who works in a pharmacy as a clerk. What does she have to offer you? What could she—"

"Mom, stop. You're chasing the wind."

"Huh? What are you talking about?"

"You know exactly what I'm talking about now that I think about it. That church you attend, they're all chasing wind."

Felipe Sr. knew exactly where his son was headed, and it made him unbelievably proud.

"You have such a focus on material things," Felipe continued, "so did Sandra. Anything that does not have eternal significance is just chasing the wind. What good would it have done me to stay here and deliver rich women's babies? I deliver babies to women that are on welfare, but when I'm in that delivery room, I know that by helping these women, I am serving God." He got up and stood by the sliding glass doors looking out into the yard as if to catch his breath. "In all

the years Alex and I attended church, all we s҇
pretending to be perfect, and condescendingly p
down who weren't. It's sad because they made G
someone you only went to for forgiveness. Som҇   ҉
was waiting for us to fail so we could be punished. Well, I've
discovered that they were wrong." He turned around and
looked at his parents directly. "They were wrong," he repeated.
Now I'm going to sound like you, Mom, except I mean it. In
Ecclesiastes, Solomon said that controlling the outcome of
your life, being in envious competition, and trying to make a
name for yourself, all involve chasing the wind. To quote the
Bible more directly, 'I have seen all the things that are done
under the sun'..."

"All of them are meaningless, chasing after the wind.' Ecclesiastes 1:14," Victoria chorused with her son, her eyes stinging
with tears. "Well, you've given me a lot to think about."

Felipe walked over to his mom and hugged her tightly.
"Mom, I love you. But you have to let me live my life, and
part of that includes trusting me and the decisions I make."

"I only want what's best for you and your brother. You know
that right?" she replied as she wiped her tears.

"I know," he whispered.

"Okay, now tell me about Fatima."

Felipe laughed aloud. "You're something else, Mom."

"Bueno, when do we get to meet our new daughter-in-law?"
Felipe Sr. interjected.

Felipe was grateful that the worst was over. They knew as
much as he needed them to know. He loved his mother, but
he had taken a stand. "Soon, Dad. Maybe next weekend you
can come down and have dinner with us. Mom?"

"Yes, of course. We'll come down next Saturday. I was just

about to make sandwiches for us. Stay for lunch?" It was her way of making peace.

"Of course. And I'll tell you all about Fatima," he smiled at her.

* * *

Hey wifey, going to each lunch here with my parents. See you soon, he texted Marisol.

No worries! Take your time. Sounds like it went well and I'm glad, she responded.

It did!

* * *

"You didn't answer my question," Fatima said to Marisol as they were doing their toenails.

"What question was that?" Marisol responded as she put her phone down.

"How did it go last night?"

"If you're asking me if we had sex, we did not."

"Why not?"

"Are you forgetting why Felipe and I got married?"

"No, what does that have to do with anything? You're married to him. It's fair game."

"Maybe he doesn't want to. Remember, we're friends."

"Yeah, okay. You really believe he doesn't want to? Has he said that?"

"No."

"Then?"

"What am I supposed to do? Lay in bed and say, 'come and

120

get me'!"

Fatima paused to think. "Yeah, pretty much."

"You're crazy," Marisol said, focusing back on her toes.

"You know what you need?"

"No, Fatima. What do I need?" Marisol mumbled focusing on getting her tiny toenail properly polished.

"You need a seduction plan. And you need a sexy nightgown. Not those pajamas with the monos on them."

"Hey, those pajamas with the monkeys on them are cute," Marisol protested.

"Yes, but you're trying to seduce your husband, not get him to contribute to the Bronx Zoo." Fatima went to her bag and pulled out *Cosmopolitan* magazine. "There's an entire article in there with romantic strategies to get your husband in bed."

"A sexy dessert?" Marisol said as she thumbed through the magazine.

"Keep the magazine and at least read the article."

"Okay." She stuffed the magazine under her mattress. "Now, tell me about you and Alex."

"We're doing good. It hasn't been that long since we met, but it feels like I've always known him. I can just be me and it feels right. We like doing the same things, so it's just easy. It's hard to explain."

"You don't have to," Marisol responded, feeling like she was listening to herself explain her relationship with Felipe.

* * *

I just got off the train. Picking up Fresco's Pizza, Felipe texted Marisol.

Marisol set the table for them, and as soon as he arrived

with dinner, they said grace and started to eat.

"So tell me how it went," Marisol impatiently asked.

Felipe had taken a bite of his pizza and was chewing as she impatiently waited. "She asked me first if you were pregnant."

Marisol stopped with a mouth full of pizza mid-chew. "How?"

He stared back at her. "Seriously? The usual way. You walked right into that one," he quipped picking up another slice.

"Yeah, I really did. Anyway, go on."

"After I clarified that, she went on about—" He hesitated.

"You can tell me. I knew she wasn't going to ask you if we were registered for gifts anywhere."

"Well, let's just say that she—"

"No, I want to know exactly what she said."

"She said that she couldn't envision a future between a doctor and a pharmacy clerk."

"Che stronza!" Marisol exclaimed with tomato sauce on the side of her mouth.

"That didn't sound nice," he said, trying to conceal a smile.

"It means 'that bitch' in Italian," she sheepishly admitted.

"Fair enough, and she certainly acted that way until I put her in her place," he responded as he wiped the sauce off her mouth with his napkin. "I got a lot off my chest. Stuff I had been wanting to say to her since I left Connecticut. It was a breakthrough. That's how I'm looking at it. We had sandwiches for lunch, and of course, she grilled me about Fatima. I told her she would meet her Saturday."

"Why Saturday?"

"They want to meet you and that's fair. I'd rather them come here than us go up there."

"Let's invite Rosa and Bernie too."

"Great idea. We'll set up the tables in the living room like we did last night. Bernie can bring the folding chairs we used in the summer for the picnic. So what did you do today?"

"In the morning I did laundry and ironed. I ironed your shirt for church tomorrow and your scrubs."

"You didn't have to do that. I know how to iron."

"I told you laundry and ironing are mine."

He put his hands up to show he understood. Hands off.

"Then, in the afternoon, I hung out with Fatima."

"How are they doing? I haven't talked to Alex about what's going on with them."

"They're doing good. Just enjoying each other with no stress. I talked to Rosa on the phone after Fatima left."

"How did that go?"

"It was fine. She suggested I take half a day on Monday." She twitched her nose.

"You're twitching your nose. What are you not telling me?"

"Nothing," she lied.

"Oh, come on. I told you everything."

"Okay, okay. She asked me what I was doing for birth control."

"And you said what?"

"I said, I said that we—I told her not to worry about it. That we're still talking about it."

"And are we?"

She smiled at his advance. "You tell me. Are we?" *Did I really just say that aloud?* she asked herself.

The sharp knocking at the door startled them both. They laughed and Felipe went to answer the door as Marisol cleaned up the kitchen. He came back with a box of cookies.

"Who was it?"

"Orlando's daughter selling Girl Scout cookies."

"Nice. I'll make some coffee."

* * *

Marisol read the *Cosmopolitan* magazine Fatima gave her and Felipe watched an intense college basketball game. During a commercial, he looked over at her and noticed she was smiling as she mouthed the words she was reading.

"Interesting read?" he asked.

"You could say that," she smiled. *And ever so handy. Perfect timing, Fatima.*

"What are you reading?"

"Nothing," she responded, nose in full twitching mode. "It's a wine recipe."

"Liar," he smiled.

"It is," she innocently replied. She switched to a different part of the magazine. "See? Anyway, I'm going to bed."

"Hey, I have to go by the hospital after church tomorrow. Come with me. I'll introduce you around."

"Okay."

He shut the TV off. She was walking into her room when he gently grabbed her arm and pulled her in for a hug. "It's going to be okay. I know that the past forty-eight hours have been surreal, but each day that goes by is one more under our belt."

She looked up at him and they locked eyes. He kissed her lightly and tenderly on the lips. "Good night, Colu—I mean Ortega."

"Good night, Ortega," she replied. She slowly turned around and closed her eyes.

I missed my cue. I should have just ripped off my clothes.

"Hey," Felipe called from his room.

"Yeah?"

"We didn't pray. I will this time."

"Go for it," she encouraged.

"Hey, God," he began.

She smiled at his familiarity with God.

"Thank you for this day. Thank you for the blessings you provide for us. Food, a roof over our heads, and your guidance. Keep us focused on your plan and guide us through the coming days. In Jesus' name."

"Amen," they said together as was becoming their custom.

Chapter 12

"Ah the Ortegas," Pastor Melvin greeted Marisol and Felipe as they were leaving the sanctuary. "I ran into Bernie yesterday at the bodega and he told me the good news. Once you are settled, I would love for you to say your vows again, but in church. I hope you didn't mind me introducing you to the congregation as newlyweds."

"No, of course not. It's okay, Pastor," Felipe reassured him.

"Thank you, Pastor. It was very sweet of you," Marisol added.

"The Ortegas!" Dolores, one of the church members, exclaimed. "You look so adorable together and you're going to make beautiful babies!"Felipe looked straight at Marisol and smiled at her turning crimson red. They left the church and started walking toward the train that would leave them across the street from the hospital. Felipe ran his errands and introduced his wife to anyone that had breath in their body. After a quick lunch, they went home to strategize the next step in their plan.

Chapter 12

***

"Okay, so let me ask you something," Marisol stated as she hung her sweater when they got home.

"Ask me anything," he kidded.

"I was thinking about what Dolores said and—"

"Oh, about us making babies?" he teased.

"Yes. No. Well, kind of. Let's pretend that we weren't friends. Just married."

He smiled at her logic.

"If I was pregnant, would you be my doctor?"

"No way. There would be a conflict of interest. Because you're my wife, I would want to be there as your husband and the dad. If I were your doctor, I couldn't do that."

"Makes sense," she smiled.

"Okay, let's talk about tomorrow and what we need to do next." They sat at the kitchen table with the calendar.

"Tomorrow I'm going to change my name on my ID."

"And I'm going to put you on my insurance. You should get a physical as soon as you're added. A complete physical." He was in full doctor mode.

"What do you mean?"

"I mean urine, blood, mammogram, and a pap smear."

"I can do the first two, but I don't have a doctor for the last two."

"I can recommend someone."

Great. He hasn't seen me naked and the first man to see me naked will be a stranger. Unless... "Okay, but I would like a female."

"That's fine. Alex is going to meet with us soon to fill out some paperwork and prepare us for the interview with immigration. He has some contacts he's going to tap into to get it scheduled soon." They put their respective schedules on the calendar and tidied up the kitchen table.

"So I'm going to take a bath," Marisol announced. Without saying another word, she got up and headed to the bedroom. She had stuffed the *Cosmopolitan* issue underneath her bed and gently pulled it out to consult the final details for her plan. *I don't really have anything sexy to wear. But even if I did, what if he flat out doesn't want to? But maybe he does.* Then it occurred to her to test the waters, so to speak. She put the magazine back in its secret location and made sure she got everything she needed. Everything except her towel.

She filled up the tub and mixed in too much bubble bath, which made the water very soapy and the tub slippery. Marisol kept a small radio in the bathroom which she turned on to the oldies station. She put one foot in the tub and slipped a little but balanced herself with the wall and carefully sat in the tub. She sang along with Rod Stewart's "Do Ya Think I'm Sexy."

"If you want my body and you think I'm sexy, come on baby let me know," she belted from the top of her lungs as she shaved her legs. First the right. Then the left.

Felipe paused the TV. *If I want your body? You bet I want your body. Easy, cowboy. It might just be a random song.* He started the TV up again.

Singing sexy song. Check. Bubbles up to the neck. Check. Now, I just have to drape my leg over the tub. She proceeded to follow the last of the instructions but placed her leg too far out. Because the tub was so slippery, she ended up gently falling back and submerging herself completely underwater. She sat up with her hair looking like a mop that needed desperately to be wrung out. *Smooth, Colucci. Ortega. Whatever. Now what? Think, Marisol, think.* She looked around to see if by chance there was a towel she could at least wipe her face with. Nothing. She rinsed her face and reorganized her hair as best she could. Making sure the bubbles were up to her neck, she thought, *Okay, here goes nothing.*

"Felipe," she called out.

"Yeah?" he responded.

"I forgot my towel. It's on a hanger on my closet door. Can you bring it to me?"

He put his soda can down on the end table and paused the TV. He picked the towel up off the hanger and knocked on the bathroom door.

"You can come in." He walked in and there she was with her long leg hanging over the tub like a snake.

"Check you out covered in bubbles." He hung the towel on the rack and proceeded to sit on the side of the tub.

Grab him and pull him in. I dare you. I'm not ready to do that. The article didn't say anything about that, she argued with herself.

"You're nodding your head again, so I imagine your thoughts have overtaken you." He brushed one hair away from her eyes and left the bathroom.

Well, that was an epic failure. She sighed. She tried to incorporate herself into the tub only to fall back and end up underwater all over again.

* * *

The next morning, Felipe rolled over and looked at the clock. "Marisol?" No response. Looking around the apartment, he realized she had left early. Walking into the kitchen to get some coffee going, he noticed a note on the counter.

Felipe,

You were sound asleep when I left. Did not want to text so that the phone would not wake you. The coffee is all set up and ready to brew. I am going to work after I'm done with the paperwork to change my name. I also packed your dinner. It's in the fridge next to my water bottle. I'll text you when I get to work.

Your wife,

Marisol

He smiled at the happy face as if it were her sweet smile that was looking back at him. He took his coffee into the living room and was about to pick up the remote control when he noticed the pictures she had on the wall. He had seen them before, but it was the first time he really looked at them. There was a family picture of Marisol with her parents and brother, another one with her and her mother, and still one more with Marisol and Anthony. He tried to decide who she looked like. She definitely had her mom's smile and hair. But those big brown eyes were her dad's. How he wished he could reassure them all that she was okay. That he would always take care of her. It suddenly occurred to him that when he proposed his plan to her, neither one of them broached the subject of what they would do once everything was taken care of. An annulment? A divorce? He teared up just thinking about it.

I'm such an idiot, he said aloud, and he thought back to his brother asking him if he was in love with his wife. *I hate it when my brother's right.*

* * *

"I'm here," Marisol announced as she walked through La Esquinita.

130

"Thank God you're here. My mom went home to have lunch with my dad, and I was bored. How did it go last night?"

"Horrible. Give me a minute. I promised Felipe I would text him when I got to work." She stood behind the counter with a half-smile on her face as she typed her message. She put her phone away and gave Fatima her undivided attention. "It was a disaster. I put too much bubble bath in and almost ended up drowning myself."

"Oh no."

"Oh, I pretty much recovered from that one. He came in and sat on the edge of the tub."

"Please tell me you yanked him into the tub with you."

"No, but I thought of it!"

"Marisol!"

"Well, he did hug and kiss me good night."

"Ooh. He kissed you good night. Please don't tell me you had the monos on."

"Of course I did. I was going to sleep."

"That wasn't the plan. You're scared, aren't you?"

"Of course I am. I've, you know, never done it. And I don't know if he wants to."

"Trust me, he wants to. He just doesn't want to pressure you. And if you don't want to, that's another story. But I know you want to."

"I do. Anyway, I'm going to try the dessert one tonight."

"Let's get you something to wear for the occasion. We'll go shopping when we get out of here."

"Fine. Hey, before I forget, Felipe and Alex's parents are coming for dinner next Saturday night. I called your mom this morning."

"That should be fun."

"Hey, you need to make a good impression. She'll be your mother-in-law someday too," she teased Fatima.

* * *

The hospital had been quiet for a Monday night. Felipe was heating up the dinner Marisol had packed for him. Watching the microwave timer tick off the seconds put him in a trance as he thought about the last three days.

"There's the newly married man!" Bernie was walking in with his dinner.

"Hey! I know Marisol is going to let Rosa know, but you're coming over for dinner on Saturday night. My parents are coming up from Connecticut too."

"Nice. How did it go with them Saturday?"

"It went okay. My mom started out with her snippy comments, but we worked everything out." He was digging in his lunch box for the fork when he found a note. *Enjoy your dinner!* He smiled at her happy face.

"Good news?" Bernie asked as if Felipe had been reading the newspaper.

"Marisol wrote me a note."

"Looks like married life agrees with the both of you."

Felipe blushed and nodded. "Yes, it does. I added her to my insurance today and I want her to get a complete physical."

"Have her go to Tomas Menendez. He's really good and close by."

"That's who I was thinking of, but she wants a female doctor."

Bernie smiled sympathetically because he suspected the reason why. "Well," he started, "sometimes when young women haven't been sexually active for long or at all sometimes there's security in seeing a female doctor." Only years of wisdom would have shed that light.

Oh. My. God. Is it possible that Marisol is a virgin? Of all the things we've talked about, we've never discussed our sexual past. It hit Felipe like an atomic bomb when he put the pieces together.

"Hello? Where did you go, bro?"

"I was just thinking about how overwhelming it is for Marisol right now. Alex told me that we're still not out of the woods."

"One day at a time," Bernie gently said. "What do you want us to bring on Saturday?"

"A hungry stomach."

"That's easy."

They enjoyed the rest of their meal with a debate about the ongoing football season, the upcoming holidays, and how the weather was really getting cold. A quiet evening at the hospital was rare, so they took full advantage.

* * *

Marisol entered the apartment laden with packages in her arms. She reached her room and placed them all on the bed. She proceeded to the kitchen where she found a note from Felipe.

Marisol,

I hope you had a great day. Thank you for fixing my dinner! I'll see you later. Don't worry about waiting up for me. I know you work tomorrow.

Felipe

Not wait for you indeed, she fiendishly said aloud. *Wait til you see what I have up my sleeve tonight, buddy.* She took all the fixings she had bought to make a late-night snack to share with him. Something healthy, but at the same time sexy. Placing everything in the fridge, she spent some time organizing so it would be smooth sailing.

She went back to her room and took out *the Cosmopolitan* magazine that she had placed between her mattress and the boxspring. She flipped to the page she had dog-eared and read it aloud. "Make sure that your attire is casual but provocative." She took out her new "laid-back come and get me" pajamas. A bright red silky tank top with matching black pants. *Check. Okay, the stuff for the snack is in the kitchen.* She took a picture of the recipe to have handy and proceeded in getting ready. Radio on. Check.

A few hours later, she was in the kitchen getting things ready when Hot Chocolate's "You Sexy Thing" came on. *Perfect,* she thought.

He was about to put the key in the door and stopped when he heard singing. He smiled wondering what he was walking into. He locked the door behind him and walked down the hall.

Okay. This is it. He's home. You've got this, Ortega. Remember, the article said smooth and aloof. Whatever that means. "I believe in miracles, where you from, you sexy thing, you sexy thing you." she sang. Sensing his presence at the entrance of the kitchen. she added dancing to her performance.

"Hey, sexy," he said.

"Oh, you're home," she said casually as she turned around. She started walking over to him to greet him when her new bedroom shoes slipped on the tile floor landing her into a semi-lunge which she quickly turned into part of a dance move to save face. *That was close, but nice save* she said to herself. "So I baked a snack," she said, taking the serving plate with the sad-looking muffins that had somehow burnt a little in the oven. She placed them on the table and opened the fridge for the whipped cream. "Are you going to shower first?" she asked.

"These look good," he bluffed. "Let's eat now and then I'll shower."

"Great! So have a seat." She had set the table up with coffee cups, creamer, and little plates for their snack. Felipe took his seat as Marisol began to struggle with the nozzle of the whipped cream can.

"I'll get that for you," he said offering assistance.

"No, no. I've got this." She turned the can around to inspect what was wrong and pressed hard again. This time, the nozzle got stuck, spraying whipped cream all over her hair, new outfit, and the floor. In her desperate attempt to stop it, she turned the can around and covered Felipe. Since he was dressed in green scrubs the whipped cream made him look like an overdressed Christmas tree. Whipped cream everywhere except on the muffins.

Marisol stood there mortified, fighting back the tears and looking like Frosty the Snowman.

"It's okay. It's okay," Felipe said laughing, "it's just whipped cream," he tried to reassure her not understanding what had gotten into her.

"I really wanted this to be a surprise."

"It's okay," he kept saying to comfort her as he used paper towels to clean himself off. "You go take a shower."

"No, you go first. You just got home from work."

"Marisol, you've got that stuff buried in your hair. Go. I'll

135

shower after."

"Okay," she said meekly. As she was walking out of the kitchen, she slipped on the whipped cream and fell on her butt. He helped her get up and she went to take a shower.

She came out in her sweats and the kitchen looked the way it did when she first got home. "You're incredible. I made the mess. I should have cleaned it up," she said as she dried her hair with a towel.

"And risk having the whipped cream sit in your hair? No way. Okay, I'm going to go shower now. When I get out, we'll eat the muffins."

"Okay." She waited until he was in the shower and could hear the water running. She called Fatima.

"I'm guessing since you're calling me that things did not go well."

"It was an epic whipped cream disaster. I'm sorry I'm calling you so late."

"It's okay. What happened?"

"You mean aside from me embarrassing myself? I don't understand what's going on with me."

"You're trying too hard. Just be yourself. Forget about that magazine. He fell in love with Marisol. Not Marisol trying to be someone else."

"If you say so. The water just went off. I'll see you tomorrow." She remembered that she had left the magazine on her nightstand. The double doors were wide open and as she was about to walk in, he was coming out of the bathroom in shorts and a tank top. *My humiliation will be over the top if he sees that magazine. But if I walk too fast, he'll see me. If he just looks over there, he'll see it. Okay. Deep breath. Be myself. That's what I have to do.* He was whistling to get her attention.

"I'm sorry, what did you say?" she said coming out of her trance.

"What's gotten into you?"

"What do you mean?"

Shaking his head, he responded, "You're just not yourself. It's almost as if—" He did not even finish the sentence when he saw it. The magazine. The bright red letters which screamed, *come read me for advice.* He looked over at her and then the magazine again.

She darted her eyes toward the dreaded corner and then back at him. As if the theme from *Mission Impossible* played in the background, they both lunged for the magazine. Marisol reached it first and plopped herself on the bed on top of the magazine with Felipe over her trying to pull the magazine out.

"Come on. Give it up."

"No."

"You leave me with no other option." And with that, he started to tickle her. She laughed until she was almost breathless.

"Okay, okay."

"Are you going to give it up?"

"No, but we do need to talk," she negotiated. He moved away from her with a smile. She put the magazine face down out of sight tucked in its proper quiet place. She turned around and he extended his arm.

"Ladies first," he said politely.

She walked into the living room turning around to make sure he was following. She picked up a cushion and hugged it as she made herself comfortable on the couch. He sat down facing her, and as he did, she caught a whiff of his cologne, which made her heart do the paso doble.

"Seriously, what's going on with you?"

"Okay." She sighed and started nodding as if she were putting her thoughts in an order that would make sense. "Okay."

"I'm not in your head, hon. What's happening?"

She melted like an overcooked grilled cheese at his endearment. *He called me hon. Okay, you've got this.* "Okay."

"You've established it's okay and I agree. Come on. Spill."

"So I really want to…hmmm. What I've been trying to unsuccessfully do is hmmm" She closed her eyes and the words tumbled out of her. "I was thinking. We're married and I'm not sure where you are with 'this'."

"What is 'this'?" he asked following suit with air quotes. And then it hit him. *She wants to have sex.* "I don't want to be presumptuous, but are suggesting that we consummate this marriage?"

She was nodding her head affirmatively with eyes shut and sporting a big smile in appreciation of his understanding.

"I've wanted to, but I didn't want to pressure you."

"I mean, we're married. We might as well reap all of the benefits, right?"

He laughed at her choice of words. She was straightforward most days and it's one of the many things that had made him fall in love with her.

"But there's something else," she whispered as she started fidgeting with the cushion again. "So I really haven't—you know, for some people—" She started to babble.

"Why are you whispering?" he asked.

"Am I?" she whispered.

"You are. As if you're trying to tell me a secret. Are you trying to tell me you're a virgin?" he whispered back.

She nodded her head yes as she stared at the floor. That was it. Everything was out in the open. Well, almost everything. She stood up and lowered the radio a little more. "I didn't want to just come out and say, hey, want to have sex? So I thought if I sent you signals, you might, you know. I found an article in that magazine that provided tips on how to seduce your husband. You know Felipe, I started to think that if I took off all my clothes and stood in front of you, you wouldn't know what to do with me."

She watched as he walked over to her and remembered the magazine's suggestion to have a glass of wine to relax. *One glass. Forget it.* She desperately picked up one of the wine bottles and started gulping with desperation.

"What are you doing?" he asked her as he was smiling and frantically trying to take the bottle away from her.

She stopped long enough to inform him. "It's just to relax me. You know," she continued guzzling as he was grabbing the bottle.

"Stop. Stop. Marisol, it's not a death sentence." He put the bottle back on their makeshift bar. The song "Hero" by Enrique Iglesias started to play. Felipe put the volume up maintaining the intimacy of the moment he was about to create.

"Dance with me. Just like we did last Friday. "He took her in his arms and just tenderly held her as they swayed back and forth. *Would you swear that you'll always be mine? Or would you lie? Would you run and hide? Am I too deep? Have I lost my mind? I don't care, you're here tonight.* He serenaded her, and she started to relax. "You always smell so good."

Eyes shut, she smiled.

"There's something I have to tell you as well," he continued. "I am totally and completely in love with you." The music continued, but they stopped dancing. He locked eyes with her. "I love you, Marisol Ortega. I want to be married to you for the rest of my life. I want to have children with you. I don't care what people say about how long we've known each other. I know what I want and it's this." He brushed a tear away from her face as he choked back his own. "What do you say about that?"

"I love you too. So much," she said through the river of tears that were now streaming down her face. They continued dancing long enough to compose themselves.

"What if I'm deported?" she whispered.

"Alex says we have a huge battle ahead. But we will deal with whatever comes our way. And, if it comes to that, I'm going with you and we'll figure things out in Honduras. But together." The song ended and they stopped dancing. He pulled her chin up to his face and kissed her. Sweetly and passionately. He scooped up his wife in his arms and they headed to the bedroom.

Chapter 13

"Y"ou know what I've always wondered?" Marisol asked
as she contentedly lay in his arms with her head on
this chest.

"What?" he asked as he played with her hair.

"You know how if you work at a bakery, for example, the
last thing you want to see when you get home is cake."

He smiled because he knew where she was going.

"So you look at women's private parts all day. Isn't it the last
thing you want to see when you get home?" She looked up at
him.

"Well, that depends."

"On what?"

"Whether the cake owner is offering a whipped cream
special."

She smiled at his teasing. "No, I'm serious."

"When I'm delivering babies or seeing patients, I'm looking
at that part of their body the same way a different specialist
would look at the body. It's just science to me."

She nestled her head on his chest again. "I have another question."

"Of course you do."

"Am I the first person you've slept with that had no experience?"

"Are you asking me if you are the first virgin I sleep with?"

"That word is no longer a part of my vocabulary," she said smiling as she wiggled her toes.

"You are. And I have not one regret. The question here is were you disappointed?" Marisol wiggled her toes again as she responded, "No," with a smile from ear to ear. Until she realized something was wrong. She sat up in bed and looked at him.

"Felipe, you're on the wrong side of the bed."

"Excuse me?"

"I sleep on the right side of the bed. That's if you're facing the bed. If you're not facing the bed, it's the left." She lay back down.

He sighed, "Ay Marisol," and as he started to move across her, he gently lay atop of her with his elbows on the bed enabling him to look at her face to face.

"Well, as long as you're here, you know what they say, right?" she asked.

"More pearls of wisdom?"

"Practice makes perfect."

He kissed her and whispered, "I couldn't agree more."

* * *

Marisol's phone alarm went off. She shut it off and, realizing she still had an hour before she had to get ready, she rolled over.

Felipe was sound asleep. *Heavenly Father, what a blessing you've sent me in this man. How I wish Mami, Papi, and Anthony were here to meet him. Dad would have loved him, and he would have been like a brother to Anthony. Thank you for Rosa and Bernie and Fatima. Thank you for every blessing that you provide for me. Your word says to ask for wisdom and discernment. Please provide us both with it. Give us guidance to take care of each other and always place our marriage first. In Jesus' name. Amen.* She got up and caught her reflection in the mirror. She had forgotten to put her hair up before she went to sleep, and she looked like the scarecrow from the Wizard of Oz. She hurried to the shower.

She was doing her hair when Felipe walked in to use the bathroom.

"Good morning," he mumbled half asleep.

"Hey sleepyhead. Why are you up so early?"

"I wanted to see you before you left." He stood behind her and hugged her. Looking at their reflection in the mirror he couldn't help but notice how good they looked together. "

* * *

They ate breakfast and Marisol left for work. It was around 11:30 that Felipe went downstairs to get the mail. Three pieces addressed to Marisol Ortega caught his attention. They were from Barkley Court Reports, New York Career Institute, and MGR Rep—all three schools for getting licensed in court reporting. He smiled as he remembered the first time he had heard her talk about it. The buzzing of his phone brought him back.

Hey, I'm up. Ready to help you move the rest of your stuff when you are. Alex had taken the day off so he could help his brother move the remainder of his things into what was now the married Ortega apartment.

I'm on my way up. Just came down to get the mail.

Felipe's things were in boxes, so it didn't take long to move his stuff, and their father had mailed Alex some of his stuff. Since their parents were coming for dinner Saturday night, they would bring another round of boxes.

"Let's get pizza," Alex suggested.

"Yep. I'll call it in," Felipe agreed as he was phoning it in.

It was around noon that they were finally sitting in Alex's living room eating.

"Does it feel weird to be visiting your old apartment?"

"It does," Felipe said looking around as he took a bite out of his pizza.

"How's it going? We haven't had a chance to talk alone."

"It's going well," he smiled before he added, "I hate it when you're right."

Alex raised his eyebrows trying to suppress a smile, "Bro, I knew it. You could deny all you want, but you never once in four years looked at Sandra the way you look at Marisol. And she looks at you like you freaking hung the moon."

"Yeah, I know," he responded thoughtfully.

"Don't worry about Mom and Dad. Well, Mom. Dad's cool with everything. Mom's coming around. You know that she doesn't think anything is a good idea unless it's her idea."

Felipe started laughing because he knew that his brother's assessment of their mother was right on point. "I know. And she liked Sandra a lot."

"No, she didn't," Alex retorted as he tore into a chicken wing. "She liked the idea of Sandra. She liked that you and Sandra had gone through the 'traditional'," he emphasized with air quotes, "relationship-courtship timeline."

"I guess. I don't care. Has she grilled you about Marisol the way she's grilled me about Fatima?" he asked with a smile.

"Of course she has. I haven't told her the whole story because it's not my place, but you know deep inside, Mom has a good heart, and she just wants us to be happy. Don't worry about Saturday because you know Dad reins her in well."

"So let's talk about the elephant in the room. What's the next step for Marisol?"

"I was just about to bring that up," Alex responded as he wiped his mouth. "She has to fill out the paperwork for a change of status. I can help her with that. Once it's filled out, they'll schedule her for the interview. Sometimes they do it together, sometimes individually or a combination of both. Depends on the situation. You have to remember something important. You got married with the intention of helping to solidify her pathway to citizenship. Your relationship may be genuine now, but they're not going to see it that way. What they will see is that you got married one month after you met."

"So what do we need to do?"

"Create as many memories as possible. So when they ask you questions, you have the same answers."

"What kinds of questions will they ask?"

"All kinds. I will be there to intervene if the questions are unfair or get out of hand. When we have a date for the interview, the three of us will sit and go over some of the possibilities. But just so you have an idea, they can even ask you if you've had sex." He picked up another slice of pizza before he added with a smile. "Of course it doesn't seem like that's a problem."

"Nope," his brother responded with a half-smile.

"So you said earlier that Mom was grilling you about Fatima. What did she want to know?"

"What do you think? The usual. Where is she from? What does she do? You know. Twenty questions."

"And you said what?"

"I told her she's a nice girl and comes from a good family. What's the status between the two of you?"

"We're exclusive," he smiled. "She's sweet, kind, and very funny."

"She's a trip. And she's been a good friend to Marisol and me too."

"We'll see."

Felipe looked at his phone and realized he needed to get ready for work. "I have to go." He stood and hugged his brother. "I'm so glad that you're here."

"Me too. We still have a long road ahead with Marisol's immigration status, but we're going to get through it," he said, trying to mitigate what lay ahead.

* * *

Hey Beautiful, you got some mail today, Felipe texted Marisol before he left the apartment. *I'll leave it on the kitchen table. We finished moving everything in and then Alex and I ordered pizza. I'm leaving for work now. I love you.*

Marisol had taken the morning off to run errands and was about to enter the discount store with lunch when she felt her phone vibrate with a text message. She stopped before she went in and responded. *Hi there! Just getting to the store with lunch. Glad you got everything done. I love you too and will wait*

146

up tonight.Ha! Ha!

Felipe read her response and laughed aloud as he left the apartment.

* * *

"Hey ladies!" Marisol walked in smiling like she had a watermelon rind in her mouth.

Fatima turned around and read Marisol to a T. Fortunately, the store was closed for lunch. "You had sex, didn't you?"

"Niña!" Rosa exclaimed, mortified at her daughter's crudeness. "Te voy a dar un puñetazo," she jokingly threatened to punch her daughter before she looked at Marisol with a smile and said, "Did you?"

"You better believe it!" she said and laughed.

"Finally. How was it?" Fatima inquired.

Shaking her head at Fatima's indiscretion, Rosa turned and said to her daughter, "Don't be such a chismosa." She changed the subject. "Bueno niñas, let's get back to work. Marisol, what time do you want us there on Saturday?"

"Five o'clock is good. We're excited to have everyone over."

"Mi hija, I am so happy for you. He's a good man, but you are a gem. He's very blessed to have found you. Always keep God at the center of your marriage and you will feel like this forever."

Marisol went and hugged the woman who had been like a mother to her since her arrival.

Watching the love fest, Fatima chimed in, "Bueno y yo que. What about me?"

Marisol smiled. "Get in here, you." The three stood like a little family hugging.

* * *

It was close to midnight when Marisol heard the key turn in the door. He walked into the living room and saw that she was watching reruns of *Friends* and laughing at the same exact spots he had seen her laugh at a million times before. He also noticed that she had the brochures that had come in the mail on her lap. He leaned over and kissed her hello.

"No muffins tonight for snack," she announced.

"Thank God," he teased.

"I made torrejas instead," she brightly responded.

"Oh, that's like French toast. Nice. Should I be looking out for a whipped cream can?"

She stood up and chased him back into the bedroom.

"I'm kidding! I'm kidding," he said as she playfully hit him with a pillow.

"You're never going to let me live that down, are you?"

He smiled with that smile that just hypnotized her. "Of course not. I'm gonna shower quick and we'll eat."

"Hmmm. Your stuff's already in the bathroom."

"Ahh. What a dutiful little wife." He loved to get her going.

"Watch yourself, Ortega," she joyfully countered back. Returning to her papers, she put everything away.

* * *

"I noticed you saw the brochures you got in the mail," Felipe said as they started eating.

"Yeah. I saw an ad for the schools so I thought there would be no harm in checking it out."

"Why don't you apply?"

"I'm thinking about it. They have an online program. If I go part-time and practice diligently, I can finish in two years."

"Why don't you do full-time?"

"I guess I could, but I would have to juggle it with work."

"Why would you have to juggle anything? You're not by yourself anymore. Quit and go full-time. You know I can take care of us."

"It's just too much change in a short time. I love my job and I will just feel better if I start part-time."

He nodded his head conveying understanding. "I get it. Oye, these are good," he said complimenting her fritters.

"My mom used to make it for dessert. Also, I just think I should wait until my immigration situation is taken care of."

"Speaking of which," he said before he took a long sip of coffee, "we're meeting with Alex on Friday to fill out your application for change of status. He knows some people, so as soon as that's done, he can do his part. Once we have a date for the interview, he's going to go over the questions with us."

"Okay," she nodded her head, and he could see she was tearing up.

He moved closer and put his arms around her. "Don't worry. Because no matter what happens, we're in this together. We'll do whatever we have to do. But we'll do it together. You are the half of me that has been missing and I'm not letting you go, so get used to it. And the most important thing is that we have God's sovereign hand over our lives. I believe that with my heart and soul."

Blowing her nose and feeling better, she responded, "So you think I should apply to the school?"

"Without a doubt. I think you'd make a great court reporter, and if that leads you to another interest, that's fine too." He looked into her big brown eyes and long lashes that had been drenched with tears and gently kissed her.

"I love you," she responded.

"Back at you, Ortega," he whispered.

Chapter 14

Before the foursome knew it, it was Friday. Alex had helped Marisol fill out the application for change of status. He had expedited it as best he could, and the interview was scheduled for December 1. Since Saturday night had been set aside for their dinner party, Alex suggested they meet Friday night to talk about the interview.

"Marisol and Fatima went to get food," Felipe told Alex as he came in. The brothers headed for the living room to play video games.

"So Mom has been looking at the pictures on your social media page."

"How do you know?" Felipe asked as he aggressively manipulated the buttons on his controller.

"Dad told me. I told you she'd come around. Besides, you know you're her favorite," he joked.

"No way, you're the baby. The world revolves around you," Felipe teased him.

They heard the front door open with the girls carrying the

food.

"We got food from the bodega. There's ropa vieja, white rice and black beans. We still have torrejas leftover from the other night, so we can have those for dessert. Oh, I bought a cheesecake for dessert tomorrow and some whipped cream to add to the top."

"You sure you want to battle whipped cream again?" Felipe asked as Fatima let out a giggle.

Marisol smiled and responded, "I made sure that this time, the top was okay."

"Should I not ask what's up with the whipped cream?" Alex inquired.

"A few nights ago, we were having a snack and Marisol had a fight with the can. We both ended up covered in the stuff." Felipe and Marisol both laughed at the memory while Alex just looked at them with a half-smile. He had never, ever seen his brother this happy.

They ate their dinner telling stories, relaxing, and laughing like the family they were. Marisol made coffee and they settled in the living room. It was time to get serious.

"December first sounds like it's far, but it's not. It's about two and a half months from now. I was able to get some help from a couple of people I know that work for U.S. Citizenship and Immigration Services, or as they call it, USCIS. That's why your interview was scheduled so quickly. Remember, this is just the interview. The whole process can take up to a year, but this is the biggest hurdle."

"What about the questions?" Marisol asked.

"They're of course going to ask you when and how you met. The flag of course is that you got married so quickly. And that's where the questions could become challenging."

Marisol started to wring her hands. Felipe took her hands in his.

"They can get as personal as asking you if you have been intimate."

"That's not a problem," Marisol confidently uttered and then blushed as she watched the brothers and Fatima conceal the attempt to hide their smiles.

"They can ask you questions about each other's habits, family, the list is endless. But you're going to be okay. Keep creating memories like you have been doing." He gestured to the multitude of pictures Marisol had hung up. "For now, that's all we can do."

Marisol looked over at Fatima who had been listening intently. "What do you think?"

"I think," she paused as she started to smile, "that we should turn this over to God. We've done everything we can do for now."

Marisol smiled at Fatima's use of the word "we." She had never felt so supported.

"And I also think we should seriously consider playing Monopoly."

"That's a brilliant idea," Alex agreed. The irony was not lost on him that his brother and sister-in-law had gotten married under pretentious circumstances and now were going to have to fight to prove the opposite. What he didn't know was that the situation would become more complicated.

* * *

"Okay, four houses on New York Avenue. That will be $800.00," Marisol informed her husband as she stuck out her hand for the Monopoly money. "Wait till I put hotels up." She picked up the dice and, blowing into her hands, she rubbed them together, rolled and landed in jail. Unable to roll doubles, she decided to stay in jail.

"You want to stay in jail because you are afraid to come my way. Boardwalk and Park Place await you, darling," Felipe teased.

Fatima and Alex looked on. They were in the game each owning certain properties, but not nearly advanced as the other two.

"No, I just want to give Alex and Fatima the opportunity to visit my houses, soon-to-be hotels."

"Well, it depends on the accommodations for me," Fatima teased.

"My hotels would have the most comfortable beds with the softest sweet-smelling towels. Each room would have one of my bottles of wine, complimentary of course. For food, a mix of Spanish and Italian cuisine. And, I would have homemade pies and desserts"

"With or without whipped cream?" Felipe teased while the others laughed.

"Never mind that," she stated, trying her best not to smile.

"What about you, Fatima? What would your hotels look like?"

"Oh, you know me. Everything you mentioned, but I would throw in a spa, a gym, and of course a disco," she mused at the thought.

Before Marisol knew it, it was her turn again. She threw a double, which landed her on Free Parking. She threw the dice again and landed on Pacific Avenue.

"I will be expecting you shortly, Mrs. Ortega." Felipe

taunted.

"Maybe. Maybe not," Marisol countered.

They went another round, and she rolled a six placing her exactly on Park Place. "Okay, let's see. For a hotel, $1500. Fork it over, babe."

"I got you," Marisol replied watching her money pile dwindle. They went one more round, which wiped out Alex and Fatima. It was the war of the Ortegas. *If I can just roll a three, I'll make it to the Go tile.* Marisol reasoned. She threw the dice, and as luck would have it, she rolled a one and a one, landing her on Boardwalk.

"What are the odds?" Felipe laughed and laughed.

"Stop cackling," she mumbled. She carefully handed over the money she had and took down the houses she had on her property. Conceding that the game was over and he had won, they started cleaning up. He stood to get a glass of water and kissed her on the cheek before reaching the refrigerator.

"Oye, I have to go," Fatima announced. "It's getting late, and I promised Mom I would help her make something tomorrow."

"We told them not to bring anything," Marisol responded.

"Yes, I know, but you know how she is. Bueno, I'll see you tomorrow."

"I have to go too," Alex said.

They kissed everyone goodbye and left.

* * *

"It was a good day," Marisol whispered as she lay in Felipe's arms in bed.

"It was," he agreed.

She sighed remembering the conversation over the upcoming interview.

"What's the matter?" he asked.

"Nothing. I keep coming back in my head to what Alex said about the interview."

"Don't. Matter of fact, let's pray right now. Lord, we thank you for this day and for the daily blessings you provide for us. We leave this situation completely in your hands. You know our hearts, so please guide our steps, show favor at every turn so that we can stay in America."

The word "we" again confirmed for her that she was not alone in this fight.

"Amen," they chorused together.

"I have one more really important question to ask you," she whispered. She looked up at him and said, "Is there any possibility that I could win back my houses on New York Avenue?"

He smiled and whispered back as he turned to face her, "I think that can be arranged." He pulled the covers over both their heads.

* * *

Saturday was bursting with energy. The Ortega brothers moved the coffee table into the master bedroom to make room in the living room for a makeshift dining area. Two dining room tables pushed together with another smaller table kitty-cornered seated exactly eight. They pulled chairs from Felipe's old apartment and arranged three on each side and then one at each head of the table. Marisol had seasonal candles burning and she had cleaned the apartment until it practically gleamed. She set the table with the orange, brown, and red colors that exemplified fall. They cleared the kitchen counter completely to make space for the trays of food. The only thing left to do was wait for the guests to arrive.

"Are you nervous?"Alex asked Felipe, who was flipping from one college football game to another.

"About the interview with the immigration people? Not at all."

"No, I mean tonight. Mom."

"No way. You said Mom wouldn't make a scene, but if she does, I'm ready."

"I think it'll be fine."

There was a knock on the door, which they thought was odd because their parents were never on time. Felipe stood, adjusted his pants, and went to answer the door.

"Hey!" he happily greeted his parents with a big hug. He took their coats and hung them in the closet. "Alex is in the living room. It's a little tight because we're eight, so we moved two tables into the living room." They greeted Alex, and all sat to chat.

"Where's Marisol?" Victoria casually asked.

"Across the hall at Fatima's. She went to help her do something, but she'll be back soon." He noticed that Victoria was carefully studying all the pictures Marisol had hung up. She could see the timeline that had led to her son's hasty marriage. As much as she hated to admit to herself, he looked happy. Much happier than he had ever been with Sandra. Her trance was broken by Felipe Sr.

"Is Fatima the young lady you're seeing?" Felipe Sr. asked Alex regarding a picture of the four of them at the park.

"That's her," he proudly responded. Victoria walked over to the wall that was covered with pictures and inspected Fatima.

"Marisol, be careful, you're going to drop the tray."

Felipe heard "Marisol" and "drop" in the same sentence and hurried to help.

"I've got it." Felipe intercepted her in the hallway and took the tray as she made her way into the living room.

"Hola, cómo estamos por aqui?" Marisol greeted her in-laws with a handshake and a kiss.

"Cómo estás mi hija. ¡Felicidades!" Felipe Sr. warmly reciprocated.

"Yes, Marisol, congratulations," Victoria added with a cooler demeanor. Felipe Sr. shot his wife a look that zapped her tone. "Can I help you with anything?"

"No, everything is ready. Please, sit. What can I get you to drink? We have Coke, Materba, Jupiña and—"

"And wine made by Marisol," Felipe proudly announced. He opened the bottle and poured everyone a glass.

"Hello?" Bernie called out as he and Rosa made their way into the apartment.

"We're in the living room," Fatima responded as she made her way down the hall to help them carry in food.

The Gonzalezes made their way into the living room. Introductions were made and they were each given a glass of wine.

"Bueno, I think I'll propose a toast," Felipe Sr. announced.

"Oh, oh. We might be here till Christmas," Alex said.

Felipe Sr. laughed at his son's teasing and lifted his glass. "When you have children, all you can ever hope for is that they are happy and that their happiness comes from things that matter in life. Cars, clothes, money. They all come and go. And I know many people that have spent their life chasing materialistic dreams and have ended up alone. Because it's never enough." He turned to face his son. "As much as we would have liked to have been able to be there on your special day, the two most important people were there. You and Marisol. I've never ever seen you look this happy, and for me, that's everything. Marisol, welcome to the family. Cheers!"

"Bueno, I'm going to say a few words," Bernie announced.

Fatima looked at Alex, "Christmas? Now we may have to wait until Easter to eat."

"Callese," he jokingly reprimanded his daughter to be quiet while the others laughed.

"Felipe, as you know, Marisol's parents are deceased, and for now, we don't know where Anthony is. So on behalf of my wife Rosa and myself, I would like to say a few words. Marisol is an intelligent, strong young woman, who in her young life has been through more than all of us in this room put together."

Marisol's eyes became a little glassy as her husband put his arm around her and kissed her head.

"And yet, her faith in God," Bernie continued, "has been a shining example for us. When Tomasina passed away, we offered to move her in with us. She had only been in the city for a month, but she said no. She told us that she would never be alone. That God had never abandoned her. She has become like a daughter to us and a sister to Fatima. The three of us," he continued as he pointed to his wife and daughter, "watched the relationship between these two develop and grow. Was I surprised with their marriage? Yes and no. Yes, because like you, we would have wanted to be there. But no, because we knew they were in love with each other before they did."

Marisol and Felipe gave each other a confused look tainted by a slight smile.

"Yes, we did," Fatima added, "But está," she pointed her thumb to the right indicating she was referring to Marisol, "was stubborn. I knew she loved you way before you were married."

"Fatima!" Marisol exclaimed as Felipe suppressed a grin.

"Fatima," Alex chimed in, "my brother was in denial too. No worries."

"I don't think I was done," Bernie interrupted.

"Dad, the arroz con pollo is getting cold," Fatima pointed out.

"I'm almost done. Always put God first in your lives like you have been doing and you will always look at each other the way you do now. To Felipe and Marisol."

"The wine is very good, Marisol. You'll have to show me how to make it sometime." It was Victoria's way of reaching out.

"Of course," Marisol responded warmly. "I would love to."

Rosa saw this as an opportunity. "Marisol, can I show Victoria the wine room?"

"I was just about to suggest that so Fatima and I can start heating up the food," Marisol responded.

As far as Rosa was concerned, Victoria having an issue with Felipe's abrupt marriage was on her, but there was no way Marisol was going to get caught in the crossfire. *Okay, let's handle this with finesse* she told herself as she closed the door.

* * *

"Wow," Victoria said as she looked around, "how did she learn how to do this?"

"I'll tell you in a minute. I wanted to speak to you alone.

Mother to mother," Rosa said as they settled themselves at one of the tables.

Victoria's face went from concern, to shock, and eventually, tears as Rosa poured out Marisol's story. She knew it was a gamble. But she also knew that Victoria would not do anything that would jeopardize her son.

"So you see, she's like a daughter to us." Rosa walked over to a crying Victoria and put her arm around her. "I didn't tell you this to upset you or to have you feel sorry for her. I wanted you to know because she is a good girl, and if I had a son, your son would not be married to her now," Rosa teased.

Using her napkin to blow her nose, Victoria composed herself before she responded. "I didn't come here today to cause trouble."

"I know you didn't." *But just in case, you're on notice*, Rosa thought.

"I do want to get to know her, and to be honest, I've never seen Felipe this happy."

"And I was really glad that you reached out to Marisol asking her to teach you how to make wine. And she will. Now, can I ask you a question?"

"Of course."

"Do you have the 411 on Alex and Fatima?"

Both mothers laughed and hugged.

Chapter 15

"Okay," Felipe announced, "the food is in the kitchen, and we've set it up buffet style. Everyone serve yourselves, we'll say grace and then eat."

Felipe sat at one end and Marisol at the opposite end. Felipe Sr., Victoria, and Alex on one side, and Bernie, Rosa, and Fatima on the other.

They were about to say grace when Felipe Sr. blurted, "Ay caramba, I left my camera in the car." He started to get up.

"Psst. Oye, Dad," Alex whistled to get his attention, "look, we have cell phones," he said waving his. "We can take pictures and print copies for you."

"Pero, my car is right downstairs."

"Felipe, the food is served," Victoria pointed out.

"Bah. Okay," he responded.

"Felipe, you say grace," Marisol instructed with a smile.

"Yes, dear," he jokingly responded, as her smile got wider. "Heavenly Father," he sighed, deeply relieved that the evening was progressing smoothly, "we come before you in complete thanksgiving for this family gathering and for the food we are about to eat. Thank you for this meal and for your sovereign hand that is always over us. And I especially pray that my pager does not go off tonight." Everyone let out a small laugh. "Amen."

"Alex, please take a couple of pictures," Felipe Sr. insisted.

"Yes, Dad," his son sighed and acquiesced to the request.

They had been finished with dinner for about five minutes when Marisol caught a break in the conversation.

"Okay, who's ready for dessert?" she teased. All hands went up. "Ladies, I need some help."

Felipe Sr. saw this as an opportunity. "Ay, I'm going to go get my camera," he stubbornly announced. "I'm old-fashioned that way, Bernie. I like to take the pictures myself and then develop them. My wife says I'm a dinosaur."

The others laughed and Victoria waved him off with a smile as he left the apartment.

Rosa, Victoria, and Fatima were bringing in the coffee pot, mugs, creamers, and eventually the apple and pumpkin pies. They came out single file with Marisol at the end of the line holding a can of whipped cream and looking like Arnold Schwarzenegger in Rambo.

"Who wants whipped cream?" she asked as Felipe, Fatima, and Alex ducked under the table simultaneously. "Ha, ha. Very funny. There's nothing wrong with this bottle. But just in case, I'll go stand by the window." She walked over as she started to struggle. "It's always just—hard," she spoke as she was fighting with the can.

Victoria walked over. "Let me try," she said.

"Oh look! I got it," Marisol exclaimed. As she felt her right-hand twist off the top with force, causing her left hand to jerk forward and toss the can out the window and right on Felipe's dad as he was making his way back into the building. "Oh no. What have I done?" she whispered, although her mother-in-law heard.

Victoria looked down, looked at her husband who was rubbing his head, looked back at Marisol. "Meh, se l'è meritato. He deserved it," she repeated for the benefit of those that did not speak Italian.

"Non è un buon modo per fare una buona impressione," Marisol responded without missing a beat.

Did she just say 'not a good way to make an impression' in perfect Italian? Victoria asked herself. The two women locked eyes and started laughing. "Don't worry about it," she reassured Marisol.

"Anyone lose a can of whipped cream?" Felipe Sr. joked as he walked back into the living room still rubbing his head. Felipe, Fatima, and Alex all pointed in Marisol's direction as Victoria winked at her daughter-in-law.

"Marisol, we didn't mean to throw you under the car," Fatima said when she was finally able to stop laughing.

"Under the bus," Marisol and the brothers chorused as they corrected her.

"You know what I meant."

"That's okay, mi hija. I needed to have some sense knocked into me," he quipped as he put his arm around Marisol.

"See!" Victoria exclaimed. "I told you," she reminded her daughter-in-law as she started laughing again. Marisol laughed and took the can back and started shaking it.

"Okay, seriously, who wants whipped cream?"

"Babe, I've got it," Felipe quickly volunteered.

* * *

"We had a good time," Felipe told Marisol as they cleaned up and debriefed the evening.

"We did, and your mom was shocked when I responded to her in Italian."

"I told her your dad was Italian, but I think it may have been when we went through that 'I'm not listening to you right now' phase."

"She was great tonight. I guess I expected her to rake me over the coals."

"That was not going to happen here because I would have not tolerated it."

"She actually wants me to teach her how to make wine."

"I know! We've got all the family issues worked out. Once we're done with the immigration interview, we're in for smooth sailing."

She nodded her head in agreement as she took his hand. They both looked around the living room and realized that they were done, so they headed for bed.

* * *

By mid-November, the Ortegas had settled into domestic bliss. Felipe continued working at the hospital and Marisol was working and getting ready to start her first semester at Liberty University's online program. They had gone to Connecticut to visit Felipe's parents and went a couple of times with Fatima and Alex. Victoria had come to the city to spend a day with Marisol, Fatima, and Rosa to learn the art of making wine. Alex and Fatima were starting to get serious and both Victoria and Rosa wondered if they would be following in Felipe and Marisol's footsteps.

Their busy schedules made weekdays challenging, but they made the best of the weekends. Life was good, but Marisol's immigration interview lurked in the shadows. They had done their due diligence filling an album with pictures that they had planned on taking to the interview. But Thanksgiving would come first, and it was a welcome distraction to be planning for the holiday.

It was the Friday before Thanksgiving, which was still Felipe's weekday off, and he was watching television when Marisol came home from work.

"Hey, how was your day?" Felipe asked as he stood up to kiss her.

"I'm sooooo relieved that we finished the inventory project before next Thursday. I am exhausted." She took off her shoes and laid on the couch with her feet on his lap.

"Well, it's Friday, and you have over a week to rest up."

"I can't believe you and Rosa talked me into taking time off."

"You need it," he insisted.

"How was your day?" she asked.

"It was good. I talked to my mom today and of course, she asked about you. Then I just hung out. I did laundry and cleaned the apartment."

"Felipe!"

"You needed a break and I'm perfectly capable of helping my wife. Remember that we're a team."

"But you worked until one o'clock in the morning last night."

"So? I didn't say I was up at five a.m. cleaning. Why don't you take a nap and then we can eat?"

"That's a good idea. But I'll just stay here," she said with her eyes closed.

* * *

She felt his finger caressing her cheek and opened her eyes. "How long did I sleep?" she asked as she sat up.

"It's six. I went to La Nueva España and bought dinner. Let's eat," he lightly spanked her behind.

"I'm gonna take a shower first. Can you wait?"

"Yeah, go ahead. I'll put the food in the oven."

She got under the hot shower and it felt good. *This is what I should have done as soon as I got home.* She washed her hair, shaved her legs, and came out feeling like a new person. She brushed her hair out to let it air dry and put on her favorite jammies that were starting to fit just a little snug. *Too much flan,* she reasoned.

"What are you smiling at?" she asked her husband as she sat down to the table he had already set.

"You always come out of the shower looking beautiful. How do you do it?" he teased.

"Ah. It's in the genes," she winked. "My mother used to tell me that some women 'assumed' that once they were married, they could come out in a bathrobe and rollers." She chuckled at the memory. "I said to my mom, 'my future husband will love me as I am.' Of course, I was eighteen when I said that."

"Yeah, three years ago," he replied with a smile as a way to remind her that she was still young.

"Feels like a lifetime ago. You know, you look at me the way my dad used to look at my mom," she said with a mouth full of churrasco.

"He must have been head over heels in love with her."

"He was. And she saw the world through his eyes." She paused at the memory before she lightened the mood. "What did you bring for dessert?"

"Flan."

"Let's share one and leave the other one for another day. The holidays are coming, and I have to slow down."

"Okay. Speaking of which, I forgot to tell you before you took a nap. Next Thursday I took an on-call shift. So let's just do Thanksgiving with the Gonzalezes."

"That's fine. We can do Christmas in Connecticut."

"Great minds think alike because that's exactly what my mom suggested. I have vacation time so I can take a couple of days."

"Sounds good to me. Want coffee?"

"I'll make it. Go find us something to watch."

"Thank you."

"For what?"

"For taking care of me."

"You take care of me too. We take care of each other."

They sipped their coffee and watched *Planes, Trains, and Automobiles.*

"Want to go to the church's fall festival tomorrow?" Marisol asked as she turned the TV off.

"Yeah, that sounds good to me."

"Let's ask Alex and Fatima if they want to go. Rosa and Bernie went tonight." They went to bed and Marisol was out before her head touched the pillow.

* * *

The smell of crispy bacon sizzling in the pan woke Felipe up.

He could hear Marisol in the kitchen preparing breakfast. He looked at the clock and realized she had probably been up for a while.

"Hey, sleepyhead," she said to him as he hugged her from behind. "I figured we'd have a big breakfast before we head out. I want to stop at the stores on 181st Street before we head to Highbridge Park. I talked to Rosa about half an hour ago. She said it was awesome. They have games, food, and rides. Fatima and Alex are coming with us."

"Good. And you look much better today and fully rested."

"What's up, bro?" Felipe said into his phone. "Okay, bye. Alex and Fatima are here," he said as they walked down the hall to let them in.

"Grab a plate," Marisol instructed Alex and Fatima. "There's plenty of food and the coffee is fresh."

"It's so cold outside," Alex said as he rubbed his hands. "We walked to the corner to get some stuff from the bakery. Ooh, this looks awesome," he added as he sat down and began to serve himself. Dishes with pancakes, eggs, and toast covered the table along with mugs of café con leche.

"Oye, we need to get to the park early because it's Saturday and it's going to be jam-packed," Fatima declared as she was spreading butter on her toast.

"I want to stop at the stores on 181st before we go. Let's go there first since it's farther down."

"Okay. Hey, we're doing Thanksgiving here, right?"

Marisol looked at Felipe. "What do you think?"

"Yeah, it's fine with me. We can set up like we did the last time."

"My mom is going to make a pernil and I'm going to make Moros y Cristianos," Fatima added.

169

"I'll make maduros and a dessert. And of course, I will supply the wine."

"What are you going to make for dessert?" Alex asked.

"Hmm. That's a good question. I'm sick of pies. Maybe a cake."

"Chocolate?"

"Sure."

"With ice cream," Fatima added.

"Okay, a chocolate cake and we'll buy ice cream to have with it. Let's clean up and get out of here."

* * *

Highbridge Park runs from 155th Street to Dyckman Street and is a fifteen-minute walk from where the foursome had shopped. At fifty degrees, the temperature was seasonally cool.

"Are you feeling better?" Fatima asked Marisol as they were washing their hands in the restroom of the park.

"Yeah, I am. I think it was the bacon this morning. It tasted greasy."

"It didn't taste greasy at all. But it doesn't mean that it wasn't."

Outside, they studied the pamphlet with the events and created an itinerary for themselves. They watched a Biblical skit that traced Rebekah's faith journey. They went on rides, ate cotton candy, and walked around admiring the art exhibits from artists in the community. In the craft section, Marisol and Fatima did some early Christmas shopping. They were about to leave when Fatima spotted the apple bobbing contest.

"Let's bob for apples!" Fatima suggested with the enthusiasm of a ten-year-old.

"It's too cold," Felipe stated with Alex nodding in agreement.

"Where's your sense of adventure? I'll go first," Marisol volunteered.

The three stood next to her as she stood in line. When it was her turn, she placed her hands behind her back and dunked her face. She chased one of the apples the way a shark pursues its prey. She came up for air. "Okay, this time I'm getting it." Sticking her head a little deeper and opening her eyes wide underwater, she looked like a piranha about to clutch its prize. *I got it. I got it,* she repeated to herself over and over again until she did. She grabbed on, lifted her head up out of the water, and shook her head from side to side drenching the other two with the water that was coming out of her hair like a sprinkler system. Felipe and Alex laughed as they moved away.

"Oye!" she heard Fatima scream. "Niña, stop. You're getting us all wet."

She stopped long enough to realize she was standing there shivering with hair that felt like a wet mop.

"You're going to get sick," Fatima reprimanded.

"I don't care. That was fun. Aren't you going to do it?" Marisol asked as she wiped her hair and face.

"Nah. I got colder than I was watching you do it."

"Chicken."

"Oye, now that you said 'chicken' I'm getting hungry. Let's go eat. I'm treating," Alex announced.

"Ooh. My brother, the attorney, is treating. I'm in."

Chapter 16

They decided on a restaurant close to the apartment. Latin/Caribbean flavors defined El Malecon restaurant on Broadway, an eight-minute walk from home. "Please eat whatever you want. I'm so hungry I think I want everything on the menu," Alex said.

"Bro, let me go half and half on you with this," Felipe said.

"No, you got lunch last time."

"Buenas tardes, my name is Leonardo, and I will be your server today." He handed them menus. "Today you are millionaires."

"How?" Fatima immediately inquired.

"Ahhh. Because I have a suggestion on the menu that you are going to love, and" he looked at Felipe and Alex, "it's going to save you money. Order Parrilla de Carnes." He proceeded to show them on the menu the feast that was comprised of skirt steak, pork chops, chicken, and sausage. "It brings rice, beans, and maduros or tostones or half and half."

The four conferred and Alex became the spokesman. "Okay,

bring us two."

"Excelente!" Leonardo exclaimed as the other four smiled. "What beverages can I get you?"

"Yes, we'll have two Coronas," Alex ordered for himself and his brother while the girls discussed their choices.

"And we will each have a glass of La Mano Derecha Cabernet," Fatima ordered.

"Aperitivos?" Leonardo asked.

"What do you think, guys?" Marisol asked trying to get a consensus on appetizers.

"Let's get the one with the variety," Alex responded.

She looked at the waiter and instructed, "Si por favor, una orden de aperitivos mixtos."

"Está bien."

"Gracias."

"I still can't get over that you speak three languages," Alex said to his sister-in-law. My mom did not stop talking about you being able to speak Italian."

Marisol smiled at the compliment. "I had the best of three worlds. Going to a bilingual school had its benefits, and of course, growing up in Honduras had me speaking a lot of Spanish. My dad taught me what I like to call conversational Italian."

Their appetizers and drinks arrived, and soon after so did their food. After saying grace, they were so hungry that the chatter had stopped with each one focused on eating. That was until Felipe noticed Marisol moving her food around the plate.

"What's the matter, babe?"

"Nothing. I guess I got filled up with the appetizer."

"Maybe it was the fried calamari."

Just the mention of the calamari made her stomach twitch. "Probably. I'll be fine. It's been a long but fun day."

"Es que, you've been pushing yourself too hard and you have the interview in the back of your mind," Fatima observed.

"Well, I have plenty of time to rest up because I won't be going back to work until after Thanksgiving." The three looked over at Alex who was completely engrossed in polishing off his meal. They stared at him as he carefully piled a piece of steak onto his fork with just so much rice.

"What? I'm listening," he said as he realized the other three were staring at him.

Too full to order dessert, they asked for a box for Marisol's leftovers and went back home.

***

"Okay, let's leave for church tomorrow around 9:30 so we get good seats," Marisol instructed as she entered the building.

They parted ways with Felipe and Marisol entering their apartment and Alex going to hang out with Fatima as had become their custom before they said good night.

"Bye-bye," Marisol said as Felipe opened their door.

She entered the apartment and a sudden wave of nausea hit her like a typhoon. *Deep breath. In through the nose, out through the mouth,* she thought. *It's not working.* She turned to face Felipe.

"What's wrong?" he asked, noticing how pale she was.

She ran to the bathroom. She could feel her throat swelling with that feeling of undigested food making its way back up. Her mouth became filled with saliva, a sign that she knew what was coming. And it sure was. She was vomiting into the toilet.

"Mama, what's wrong?" Felipe gently asked.

"You don't have to see this," she cried.

"Don't be silly. You think I'll get queasy?" he asked sarcastically as he held her hair back. She continued to violently throw up and flush. Time passed between episodes and she was convinced it was over. He helped her get up.

"I need a shower," she announced after brushing her teeth.

He turned the water on and helped her get in.

"I think you were right about the calamari," she stated as she showered and he waited.

"It probably was. You need to get in bed when you get out. It could also be a virus. You haven't been yourself since yesterday."

"I think Fatima was right. I have faith that everything is going to work out, but the closer the interview gets, the more I think about it."

"Well, you're off until after the interview. Take the time for yourself."

"We'll see. Maybe I'll make some wine. Fatima is off from school already, so maybe we can hang out."

"Exactly," he agreed as she took his hand for support to get out of the shower.

He wrapped a towel around her like a little girl. He kissed her cheek and watched her put her pajamas on. He was showering while she was settling into bed. *I don't want to be sick before Thanksgiving, Lord. Please heal my body. Thank you for today. It was just so much fun to be able to be out and be carefree No work. No immigration interview to worry about. I haven't mentioned Anthony in a while because I've been distracted with my own worries. Please keep him safe wherever he is. Bless Rosa and Bernie,*

Fatima, Alex, Felipe Sr., Victoria, and of course Felipe. Lord, I thank you for sending me the man I have always dreamed of for a husband. He may not have come my way in the traditional way, but that's your way Lord.

"What are you thinking about?" she felt Felipe's whisper in her ear.

"How blessed I am."

"Funny you should say that. I was thinking the same in the shower. How are you feeling?"

"Better," she responded almost asleep. "I love you."

"I love you more," he responded as he held her close.

* * *

The rest of the weekend was ordinary with Marisol still fighting bouts of nausea and vomiting that only occurred in the evenings. It was the night before Thanksgiving. Alex and Fatima had gone to a late movie and Marisol was home watching a *Friends* marathon on one of the local channels with a box of tissues next to her.

After a long shift at the hospital, Felipe walked into the apartment exhausted. He hung up his coat and walked down the hallway and into the living room to see Marisol crying as if she had lost her best friend. She looked up, and as she waved at him, seeing him made her cry even harder.

"What's wrong?" he tenderly asked her as he went and sat beside her. "You're watching your favorite show."

"It's the one where Ross and Rachel break up and it's just so sad," she explained.

"Marisol, you've seen the entire series a million times."

"I know," she nodded in agreement. "I just never realized

how sad it is that he cheated on her," she said as she vigorously blew her nose.

"Well, he thought they were, you know, on a break."

She darted her eyes toward him. It was her 'you didn't just say that' look and he knew it. "So you're saying it was acceptable for him to do what he did because he thought they were broken up."

He sighed. "Marisol, I just got off a ten-hour shift. Delivered four babies. One looked like he needed a shave right after he was out and the other one might as well have worn boxing gloves." He looked over at her and saw she had tears again in her eyes.

"You never answered my question," she said. "Does that mean you think it was okay for him to cheat on her?"

Didn't she hear a word I said, he thought. "I don't think it was right, but he's human, right?" *Wrong answer,* he immediately thought.

"So you would do it?" she said quietly as she continued to cry.

"You know what I think?" he asked.

She shook her head no as she blew her nose.

"I think that the combination of the holidays coming, the interview, and the fact that you have not been feeling well are causing you to see things differently. If you're not better by tomorrow, you're going to have to go to the doctor."

"I had a physical already. I think it's just stress."

"We're still going to have to get this checked out if you don't feel better soon. I'm going to go take a shower."

"Are you hungry?" she asked now in full composure.

"No, I'm just gonna have a bowl of cereal after I take a shower. Maybe we can watch this week's *Chicago PD*. If you're up to it."

"Okay," she responded with a weak smile.

"Okay." He kissed her head.

She was settled on the couch with her honey tea when he came in with a big bowl of cereal and sat next to her.

"I forgot to ask you. Where are the kids?" he asked referring to Fatima and Alex.

"They went to a midnight showing."

"What'd they go see?"

"I don't know. They should be home soon. They're so cute together. It's nice to see them becoming close."

"You mean like us?" he asked as he put the bowl on the coffee table and leaned over her.

"Something like that," she smiled. "Oh my God, can you imagine if they got married?"

"I can't imagine that," he laughed.

"Ohhh, are you afraid of having two Ortega women in the same building?" she teased.

"My brother and I would be in a world of trouble," he added as he kissed her face. He pulled her into a tender kiss that was interrupted.

"Hey, we're back,'" Fatima announced as she walked down the hall. "Everybody decent?"

"The kids are home," Marisol whispered as Felipe sat back up on the couch as Marisol fixed her pajama top. "Hey, what did you finally go see?"

"Creed," Alex responded as he sat on the recliner and Fatima seated herself next to Marisol who had scooted closer to Felipe.

"Any good?" Felipe asked.

"It was," Alex replied.

Marisol looked at Fatima for her assessment. "Did you like

it?"

"Meh. It was okay."

"Wait," Marisol said pensively. "Creed was Apollo Creed's son. I remember when Apollo Creed was murdered in Rocky IV."

She's going to start crying again, isn't she? Felipe thought.

"I remember how sad Rocky was that his best friend had been killed in the ring and then that poor boy had to grow up without a father. Can you imagine the psychological damage that's done knowing that your father was killed in a boxing ring?' She was close to sobbing.

"What just happened?" Alex whispered to his brother.

"Bueno, bueno. Enough about movies," said Fatima. "Marisol, let's go pick the wine for tomorrow. Come on." She pulled Marisol off the couch and they headed for the wine room.

"Don't ask, bro," Felipe said before Alex even had a chance to say anything.

"The holidays are tough with people who are surrounded by family. She has to be missing her parents and brother."

"I know. I've thought of that too. But I'm worried about her health too," Felipe responded lost in thought acknowledging that there was one possibility he hadn't even considered. However, he kept it to himself.

* * *

"Let's take out the ones that Victoria made with you, oh, and one of the bottles that the three of us made last summer," Fatima enthusiastically suggested.

"That sounds good," Marisol responded as she blew her nose

and composed herself.

"What's wrong, girl? What happened to you out there?"

"I don't know," she tearfully responded as she started to cry again.

Fatima hugged and comforted her friend. "You've been sick for a few days and that takes a lot out of you too. You're probably also about to get your period."

"I skipped a period, but your mom told me it's probably the stress of the interview and the holidays."

"But you're using protection, right?"

"Of course we are."

"Ah, bueno. My mom is probably right."

They heard the door open and in walked Alex and Felipe.

"What wine did you pick?" Felipe asked as he walked over to his wife and wrapped his arms around her.

"The one I made with your mom and one that we made last summer," she smiled.

"Nice!" Alex said. "I have to get going. I'm tired."

"Me too. What time should we be here tomorrow?" Fatima concurred.

"Around five?" Felipe said as he asked his wife who nodded in affirmation.

After Alex and Fatima left, the Ortegas went back into the living room and started shutting off the lights.

"Let's watch the show tomorrow. You have to get up early and I'm tired," Marisol said, sounding like herself again.

"I was thinking the same," he said as he reached out and turned off the lamps in the living room.

"I'm really sorry," Marisol said after they were in bed.

"For what?" he asked.

"For being such a cry baby."

Chapter 16

"You're my cry baby," he joked, turning to face her.

She was about to respond, and he silenced her with a kiss.

Chapter 17

Marisol was organizing the linen closet when she heard Fatima and Rosa come in.

"I'm in the spare room," she called out.

"Niña, what are you doing?" Fatima questioned as she surveyed the mess on the bed.

"Organizing the holiday linens and decorations. I already pulled the Thanksgiving tablecloth and napkins. I also made a centerpiece with an old wine bottle. Where's your mom?"

"In the kitchen putting stuff away. How are you feeling today?"

"Great! I took a nice long nap this morning, so I'm ready to go! Hi Rosa," she said as she saw her come into the room.

"What are you up to?"

"Just organizing the linens. Okay, I'm ready." She instructed them to hand her the piles as she carefully arranged them in order of the holidays. She then stuffed sachets between the piles. "I'm going to make some coffee after I shower, and we can relax before the guys get home."

"Alex is running errands," Fatima announced as the other two smiled at each other.

"Mi hija, you go take a shower. I'll make the coffee," Rosa said to Marisol.

She was in the bathroom getting undressed when out of nowhere a sudden wave of nausea struck her. She sat on the toilet seat to get her bearings. *Not on Thanksgiving. Lord, please intervene. I don't want to spend the holiday hunched over the toilet.* She took a deep breath and, feeling better, got in the shower.

Even showering just took the life right out of her. Combing her hair, she had planned on blow drying it. "Forget it," she said to her reflection. She put some powder on her pale face and joined the others.

Caso cerrado, oh, oh. Marisol could hear the Cuban-American Dr. Ana Maria Polo or as they referred to her, the Cuban Judge Judy getting started on the TV. She joined Rosa and Fatima to watch. She sipped her coffee and placed the mug on the end table for what she thought was a second.

* * *

"How long has she been sleeping?" Felipe, who had just arrived home from work, asked Rosa as he walked into the living room.

"For about an hour. She took a shower and started to drink her coffee. Pero mira, most of it's there," Rosa responded.

"Felipe, she skipped a period last month, but I assured her it was probably nerves. She told me you were using protection. But—"

"I know what you're going to say because I've had the same thought. And no method is one hundred percent," he said as he lovingly stared at his wife. "I bought a pregnancy test and I'm also going to draw her blood tomorrow and run it to the lab." He looked over at Rosa who had started to laugh. "Why are you laughing?" he asked her with a smile.

"I'm laughing because usually, it's the wife that has to break the news to her husband that she's pregnant and it looks like the two of you have switched roles."

He smiled at her observation. "Last night I came home and she was in tears over an episode of *Friends* that she has seen a hundred times. And then she was just crying for every little thing."

"The one where Ross and Rachel break up?"

"How'd you guess?"

"When she first started watching the reruns, she would always skip those two episodes because they were 'too sad,'" Rosa reminisced.

"It's not just that, though. She's been really sick at night, and first I did think it was just stress. But then she started being more sensitive than she normally is," he laughed, "and I knew something was up."

"If Marisol is pregnant, you are going to make wonderful parents. You both have taken such good care of each other and I know that whatever comes your way, you can handle it. And Bernie, Fatima, and I will be there and so will your parents and your brother."

"I love Marisol in a way that I never imagined I could love someone. I was with Sandra for a long, long time and I never felt this way about her. I don't have to work on making Marisol happy. She's happy with the important things. Family. Friends. Quality time."

"She feels the same about you. You are a special man, and she is a special woman and God made it possible for you to find each other. Even if the circumstances were not traditional."

He looked at her and smiled. Bernie was too smart, and they had figured it out. But it didn't matter. They knew he and Marisol were truly in love.

Felipe leaned toward Marisol's face and gently kissed her cheek. She stirred and opened her eyes.

"You're home," she said smiling as she stretched. She looked around and realized it was just Rosa and Felipe.

"Where is everybody?" she asked.

"Fatima went with Alex to the bodega to buy bread for dinner. Bernie texted me that he had just gotten home from work and was getting ready," Rosa responded.

"And I just got home from work. I'm going to shower so we can eat when the others get back."

"Rosa, why did you let me sleep? Let's start heating food up. Felipe, I have to put your stuff in the bathroom."

"Felipe," he responded referring to himself, "is perfectly capable of getting his own stuff."

"And Rosa can start heating the food," Rosa responded following his lead.

"Well, I have to do something," Marisol insisted. She stood up and carefully walked around the tables that were in the center of the living room, making sure that each place setting had silverware and a wine glass.

Bernie arrived and helped Felipe carve the turkey in the kitchen as Marisol took pictures. Rosa directed Alex and Fatima to set up the sides on the counter. Shortly after, they were seated at the table and ready to begin with Felipe saying grace. They all joined hands and bowed their heads.

"Heavenly Father, we thank you for this gathering and for

the food we are about to eat. We thank you each and every day for what we mean to one another. Your will is perfect for us in each and every way and we ask that you give us the wisdom to hear your voice always. No matter what comes our way. In Jesus' name, we pray."

"Amen," they all chorused in and smiled until one by one they looked Marisol's way and realized that she was pouting with huge tears in her eyes.

"Honey, what's wrong?" Felipe asked her as the last one to spot her.

"Nothing," she responded between sobs. "That was just beautiful."

He rushed to her side and hugged her. "It's okay. It's okay. Vamos, start eating before it gets cold."

She nodded in agreement, as the others looked at her sympathetically.

"Marisol, when do you start school?" Alex asked, trying to lighten things up.

"The first week of January. I'm really excited," she replied with a mouth full of turkey.

"That's awesome," Alex responded.

"So Alex, how do you like living in Washington Heights?" Rosa asked.

"I love it," he responded as he winked at Fatima, who bashfully smiled.

"There are four apartments on this floor and three of them are family!" Fatima bragged.

"We own the second floor." Marisol high-fived her brother-in-law and Fatima.

"Don't look now," Felipe said, "but it's snowing." The others turned around and noticed the snow gingerly falling.

"Wait, we can see it better from our bedroom," Marisol announced. They all crowded around the window watching the snowfall. Felipe and Marisol looked at each other and remembered that fateful day they met on the fire escape. They only had to smile to know what the other was thinking.

"Who's ready for dessert?" Rosa announced.

"Me," Marisol gleefully shouted.

Rosa brought out the cheesecake, a chocolate cake that Marisol had made, and turrón, a dessert made with sugar and roasted nuts. Rosa surprised everyone with Arroz Con Leche which was one of Marisol's favorites. Felipe brewed an entire pot of coffee, and Marisol put out the creamers and the sugar, along with the mugs and little spoons.

"This is sooo good," Marisol said as she savored the rice pudding.

"The chocolate cake is really good too," Alex chimed in.

"I'm glad you like it. Put ice cream on it," she suggested.

They quietly ate their dessert, making sure they tried a little of each. Felipe was relieved that Marisol had not gotten sick and that she was able to enjoy a meal.

"We should go out and check out the snow after we clean up," Fatima suggested.

"Bernie and I will clean up. Ustedes salgan. Be careful and wear your coats," Rosa instructed as if they were children.

"I'll stay and help you, Rosa," Marisol offered.

"No, you go and enjoy yourself. I know where everything goes, so don't worry."

Chapter 18

T he foursome dressed according to Rosa's standards and out they headed. It had been many years since Marisol had seen snow and taking it in took her breath away. They decided to build a snowman.

"Okay, we have to make sure that with each ball, the snow is packed," New Englanders Alex and Felipe instructed.

"So it might be tough because it's fluffy, but—" Felipe had not finished his sentence when he felt a ball of wetness on his back. He turned to see Marisol laughing. "Did you just throw a snowball at me?"

"I did," she playfully stuck her tongue out at him.

"Run, Ortega. You're mine," he teased as he ran after her with a snowball. He caught up with her and lightly threw it on her leg and then picked her up in a bear hug. The protocol for building the snowman had been abandoned when Alex and Fatima engaged in a snowball fight of their own. Bernie and Rosa looked out the kitchen window and smiled at the fun they were witnessing.

"I'm exhausted," Marisol exclaimed as she took off her boots.

"Mama, the serving dishes are washed and put away. Bernie took the trash out and there is a fresh bag in the wastebasket," Rosa informed Marisol as she walked into the kitchen.

"You are the best," Marisol said, hugging Rosa. "Everyone is changing and we're watching a movie," she added.

"Bernie and I are going home. I have to open the store tomorrow and I'm tired. Have fun." She kissed Marisol, Fatima, and Alex goodbye. She approached Felipe and hugged him, whispering in his ear. "Call me tomorrow. Let me know if there's anything I can do, and Bernie called the lab and told them to expect the blood test tomorrow."

"Thank you, Rosa," he whispered in her ear and kissed her cheek.

"Anytime mi hijo. We love you both."

Marisol noticed the hug ensuing between Felipe and Rosa and it warmed her heart, not realizing that her life was about to take yet another turn. "Okay, what should we watch?" Marisol asked as she scanned the collection Felipe had brought when he moved in.

"Let's watch a comedy," Fatima suggested.

"Okay, what about *Christmas Vacation?*"

"That's a really funny movie," Alex said.

"Felipe?" Marisol asked.

"Yeah, that's fine." He had too much on his mind to really care. *It's a short movie, thank God*, he thought. He had not been able to speak to Marisol alone and there was much to tell.

They laughed and Marisol made popcorn halfway through the movie. Since they were all off, they agreed to have leftovers the next day and then watch another comedy.

* * *

"That was fun," Felipe said as he locked the door.

"It was, but I'm wiped," Marisol responded.

"I know you are. But there's something I have to talk to you about before we go to bed."

"Can we talk in bed?" she teased as she pulled him toward the bedroom.

He smiled and responded, "No, I'm serious."

She sat on the couch and he sat beside her.

"Okay," he started. "You know how you told me that you missed a period and Rosa said it could be nerves with the interview coming up?"

"Yes," she acknowledged.

"It made sense until you started getting sick and then a little overly sensitive."

"But I've only gotten sick at night," she responded as if she knew where he was going.

"It doesn't matter what time of the day it is. You've also been more tired than you normally are. So there's a good possibility that you're pregnant."

"But we've always used protection."

"It reduces the chances greatly, but it's not one hundred percent. So I bought a pregnancy test that you can take in the morning and I'm going to draw your blood and run it to the lab."

"You said you couldn't be my doctor if I was pregnant."

"I can't, but I never said we didn't have any perks." He immediately saw her mouth and eyes crinkle like they did when she was about to start crying. And then the ocean of tears invaded. "What's the matter?"

She shook her head and he sat closer to her.

"What is it, babe? Tell me."

"I should have been the one to surprise you and you ended up being the one to have to tell me because I'm an idiot!"

"No, no, you're not. I thought it was the stress too, including you missing a period. We've been using protection, so there would be no need for you to think you were pregnant. So if you think about it, if you are, we can tell him or her that we're unique because we reversed roles."

"I guess," she said as she wiped her face "Can I take the test now?"

"No, tomorrow morning as soon as you get up."

"Okay. What do you want to do now?" she coquettishly asked him.

"Whatever you want to do," he flirtatiously responded.

She took his hand and led him back to the bedroom, closing the door with her foot.

* * *

The alarm went off at 6:30 a.m. and Felipe headed to the living room, letting Marisol rest. *Heavenly Father, thank you for a wonderful Thanksgiving and life. I never imagined that I would ever be this happy. I know that today is going to change our lives because I am certain that Marisol is pregnant. But in Philippians 4:13, you tell us that we can do all things through Christ who strengthens us, and I believe that with every fiber of my being. No matter what comes our way, you will be there to guide us and give us strength.*

He noticed Marisol coming out of the bedroom. "I just did it. We have to wait five minutes." She sat beside him and he put his arm around her.

"I was just sitting here talking to God," he informed her.

"Oh yeah, what did he say?"

"That we can do all things in Christ who strengthens us. He's brought us this far. We've been faithful and have made him the most important thing in our lives. So, I believe with conviction that no matter what comes our way, he's going to guide us through."

She nodded in agreement. They sat silently for five minutes until Felipe looked at his phone to check the time.

"Ready?" he asked.

"Ready," she confirmed.

He took her hand and they walked to the bathroom together. They carefully approached the counter where Marisol had carefully placed the test on a piece of toilet paper. They stood side by side, Felipe with his arm around her.

"It's positive," Marisol said lightly. She turned to her husband whose eyes were glassy with tears.

"Yes, it is!" he exclaimed. He picked her up and spun her around as she laughed with delight. "I'm still going to draw your blood, so we have a confirmation."

"Oh, fun," Marisol said.

"I'll be gentle," he winked at her.

"Aren't you always?" she teased right back.

He smiled and hugged her.

They sat at the kitchen table with Marisol looking away from her arm.

"Make a fist with your hand," he instructed her as he tied a tourniquet around the upper part of her arm. He immediately spotted the vein. "Okay, take a deep breath," and as she did, he inserted the needle. With total concentration, he drew her blood. "Take a deep breath again," and as she did, he pulled the needle out, put a cotton ball on her vein, and instructed her to keep her arm folded in place. "I'm going right now to drop this off and wait for the results. I called the lab while you were in the shower and they're slow, so it's the perfect time."

"Call me when you know," she eagerly requested as he hurried to put his coat on.

"I will." He kissed her and took off.

* * *

Just got to the lab. They are running the test now, was the last text she had received from Felipe at 8:15 a.m. It was 9:30. Why had she not heard?

Come open the door. My hands are full, he texted at 9:45.

Why is he not using his key? Marisol wondered. She knew it had to be him because Alex and Fatima had gone to the Black Friday sales. She looked through the peephole. and sure enough, it was her husband. "You were supposed to call me—" she started to say until she opened the door and saw him standing there with a huge bouquet of pink and blue flowers.

"You know how hard it was to find this in our neighborhood? We're having a baby, Mrs. Ortega!"

"Oh my God!" She took the flowers as he kissed her cheek.

Marisol and Felipe walked back down the hall and into the kitchen. She reached for two old wine bottles that she kept around for crafts and started arranging the flowers as Felipe made breakfast.

"What's next?" Marisol asked.

"Well, Julia Torres was at the hospital. She says hi, by the way, and she told me that we need to make an appointment as soon as possible, but I got the prenatal vitamins for you." He took them out and placed them on the kitchen table so that she would not forget to take them daily.

"Felipe?"

"Hmm?" he responded as he looked for the frying pan.

"Are you happy about this?"

He turned around and sat next to her. He took her hands in his and said, "Of course I am. It happened a lot sooner than I had planned, but it doesn't matter."

"Oh, I know. It's just scary. You know?"

"We'll figure this out together. God allows things to happen for a reason. Besides, for all you know you're carrying a future president of the United States," he winked at her which still made her heart skip a beat. He continued making breakfast while she set up the coffee to make café con leche.

"Hello? Gente, we're back," Fatima announced as she and Alex lugged in their packages. They put their bags in the living room and backtracked to the kitchen. "I bought muffins for breakfast." Looking at the smiles on Felipe and Marisol's faces, she asked, "Hey, what's going on here? What's up with the flowers? And why are they pink and—" She stopped short to look at Marisol.

Felipe put his arm around his wife as she announced, "I'm pregnant."

"I told my mother! I knew it." She hugged Marisol. "I knew there had to be a reason for your crankiness and moods."

Marisol's smile dropped and she took on a look of confusion.

"Uh oh," Felipe said as he quickly returned to the boiling milk for the café con leche.

"I am not cranky or moody, right, Felipe? Alex? Come on, you guys. I haven't been that bad." Her voice started to break.

"I mean, I haven't been feeling well, but I haven't been a jerk either," she pleaded as she felt the tears streaming down her face.

"It's okay," Felipe reassured his wife as he hugged her. "Come on people, let's eat before the café con leche gets cold."As he was hugging her, he motioned to the other two to change the conversation.

They sat down to a spread of muffins, toast, frozen waffles, and cereal. They filled their plates and chatted about the weather and how quickly the fall had faded and left the winter center stage.

"I wonder if you'll have cravings," Fatima said to Marisol before she asked Felipe, "How soon do those appear?"

"It depends. Usually at some point between the third and eighth week of the first trimester, a spike in the second, and then they go down again as the final trimester progresses. She may not have started her cravings, but the way she eats her waffles has become something new."

The other two looked at Marisol's plate, which had a dab of syrup and one of butter.

"I eat my waffles like that," Fatima responded.

"Wait for it," Felipe added, knowing that the punch line was next.

Marisol stood and went to the fridge for the ketchup bottle. She sat down and opened it carefully, spooning out exactly half a tablespoon. Fatima and Alex widened their eyes as they looked on, mortified.

"Niña!" Fatima screamed. "You're going to get indigestion!"

"No, Fatima. Watch. I'm going to just add it to the very top because it adds a saltiness to the sweetness," she explained intensely as she made a sauce out of the syrup, butter, and ketchup combo.

"She's not done," Felipe said under his breath, but loud enough for Fatima and Alex to hear. He rubbed his chin and face as he watched his wife with a smile.

"Of course I'm not. Now, you cut the waffles into strips. See how they're a little hard?" she pointed out."So you dip them—"

"No!" Fatima and Alex shouted in unison as Felipe laughed.

Marisol looked at them as if they were crazy."What do you mean, no?" She proceeded to dunk the sweet and sour waffle chunk into the café con leche and then her mouth. "See?" she said with a mouth full of soggy waffles and a closed-mouth smile.

Fatima and Alex stared in total disbelief. Alex stood up to get more coffee and muttered to his brother, "Bro, it's gonna be a long nine months."

Felipe chuckled at his brother's prediction.

"My mom just texted," Fatima informed the others. "They're coming over. I can't wait for them to know."

"Your dad knows because he was at the hospital when I took your blood test in." Felipe said.

"Ugh, forget it. If my dad knows, so does my mom because they tell each other everything. I don't understand. You went and got a blood test?"

Marisol was shaking her head no, as she was chewing the last piece of semi-liquified waffle. "Felipe bought a home pregnancy test yesterday. So we did it early this morning. It was positive, so then he drew my blood and ran it to the lab."

"Fatima, your mom and I talked yesterday, and she suspected the same thing I did," Fellipe said.

"Where was I?" Marisol inquired.

"Taking a nap on the couch," he responded.

"But I thought you couldn't be Marisol's doctor?"

Marisol answered him. "He can't, but doing what he did was a perk," she smiled.

He smiled at her quoting him.

"You have to call Mom," Alex told his brother.

"I know. I talked to her yesterday." He looked over at Marisol. "She wanted to know specifically how you were feeling. We'll call her together later." There was a knock on the door.

"That's my mom," Fatima stated as she went to answer the door. The Gonzalezes made their way to the kitchen.

"There she is," Rosa lovingly said to Marisol as she hugged her. "You know your baby is going to have abuelitos in us."

"I know," Marisol responded. Thinking about her own parents and brother, she developed a huge lump in her throat. How she wished they were there.

Rosa took Marisol's face in her hands and kissed her cheeks.

"Sientese Rosa," Marisol said, offering Rosa her seat. "I have to go to the bathroom."

"Ay," Rosa reminisced. "I remember having to use the bathroom constantly." She looked over at Felipe. "Prepárate, this is only the beginning."

"Mama, wait until you see the weird combinations Marisol is making with food. Oh my God, can you imagine if she starts making wine again?"

Felipe felt the café con leche go up his nose as he laughed at Fatima's comment.

"Shhh," Felipe gently shushed Fatima.

"As long as she doesn't add ketchup, we're good," Alex joked.

"Ketchup," Bernie and Rosa cried out in unison with a smile on their faces.

Fatima started laughing as if she had someone tickling her

armpits. "Or—" Fatima said as she tried to catch her breath, "whipped cream," she whispered.

They heard the toilet flushing and became silent. Marisol stood at the opening to the kitchen. "You know I can hear you, right?"she asked as she slightly smiled.

"Never mind them," Rosa defended. "Fatima, let's go into the living room so you can show us what you bought."

Chapter 19

Felipe refreshed their café con leche and the ladies headed to the living room. He went back to the kitchen where Alex and Bernie were making predictions on Sunday's football game. They finished their conversation and Alex looked at Felipe.

"Congratulations, bro. I'm really happy for you both and I'm planning on spoiling my niece or nephew so get ready."

"Y el abuelo tambien. I may not be the official grandfather, but well, you know—" Bernie added as his voice became a little shaky.

"I know, Bernie. I know," Felipe reassured him.

"Are you ready for Tuesday?" Bernie asked nonchalantly.

"I think so," Felipe responded. "How will us having a baby affect Marisol's case? I hadn't even thought about that," he asked his brother.

Alex turned around to see if the ladies were still in the living room. He got up and slightly closed the door that led to the living room. "The TV is loud, and we can't hear each other," he informed them.

He sat again and lowered his voice a little. "It depends. If they really want to be hard-nosed about this, they can accuse you both of doing this on purpose. You met in August, were married by September, and now she's pregnant."

"That's sick," Felipe responded, and almost immediately the spirit convicted him. It was as strong as it had been when he had received the discernment of asking Marisol to marry him. *Do not be afraid or discouraged, for the Lord will personally go ahead of you. He will be with you; he will neither fail you nor abandon you.* He knew it was a scripture because he had read it in his devotional, but he couldn't remember where.

"Hello?" Alex snapped his fingers trying to bring him back to reality. "Where did you go?"

Felipe sighed and said, "Somewhere in the Bible it says that God will go before us and that he will never—"

"Yes, the Bible says, 'it is the Lord who goes before you. He will be with you; he will never leave you or forsake you. Do not fear or be dismayed'," Bernie said. "It's Deuteronomy 31:8."

Felipe nodded his head in affirmation. "That's right. The spirit just put that word in my heart. So I'm not going to worry."

"You can't add one more day to your life by worrying," Alex chimed in.

Felipe and Bernie looked at him, impressed.

"Matthew 6:27," Alex concluded as the other two started to laugh.

"I can see the influence Fatima's had on you," Felipe teased his brother.

"Yeah, she has. Why wasn't it like this when we were kids?" Alex asked his brother. He looked at Bernie and said, "I'm sure my brother has told you that we grew up in church. But it was never about having a relationship. It felt like people were constantly watching out for who was doing what. Waiting for God to punish them. Judgmental. Sometimes even competing with each other to see who had the nicest car, house. Whose kids were going to what colleges. It was crazy."

"Alex, it was never God. It's people who change that perception. But as long as you let the word of God be your anchor, you will never have a problem." Bernie said.

"Gentlemen," Felipe said, taking Bernie's hand and then his brother's, "I'm going to pray for us." They bowed their heads. "Heavenly Father, we thank you for this day and for the wonderful news we got this morning. We pray over this interview and we leave it in your hands. You will walk before us and bring us peace. This marriage started with a single purpose, but you know our hearts and you know how real it is." He felt tears stinging his eyes. "I thank you," he continued, "first for Marisol. She's everything to me. I thank you for my parents, brother, Bernie, Rosa, and Fatima. Thank you for constantly reminding me every day that you love us and what's important in life. We know that anything that comes our way is from you, and if it isn't you will walk before us. We thank you in the name of Jesus."

"Amen," the three men said in concert.

* * *

"Marisol, I remember you told me you were using protection, right?" Fatima asked while the three sat in the living room looking at the purchases she and Alex had made that morning.

"Ay, Fatima," her mother scolded. "Que entrometida eres

caramba!"

"I am not nosy," Fatima clarified. "I was just verifying."

"You're like a sister to me, so I will answer your question," Marisol responded. "We were, and it should work most of the time, but I guess not!" she exclaimed as she laughed.

"Mi hija," Rosa said to Marisol as the three broke the huddle. "I'm glad that you are at peace with the situation because God wants you to be. And you have a huge support system."

"And the best lawyer in town!" Fatima beamed.

* * *

They each had their plans for the remainder of the day and evening. Bernie and Rosa were having dinner with friends, and Alex and Fatima also had dinner plans with Alex's new supervisor and his wife. After the emotional roller coaster that Felipe and Marisol had ridden all day, they looked forward to an evening alone.

"Your mom was really happy," Marisol pointed out as they ended the call they had made to inform her of the coming addition to the family.

He put his arms around her and rocked her from side to side.

"Honey?" she uttered.

"Yes?"

"I'm getting nauseous." This proclamation made him stop immediately.

"Okay. I'm stopping," he smiled. He looked at his phone to check the time. "Hey, it's only two p.m. Are you up to going out?"

"Absolutely. Where to?"

"Somewhere romantic. Well, I think it is," he smiled. "Let's go downtown for dinner and then we can walk up and down 5th Avenue. If you're a good girl, I'll take you to see Santa."

"Let's do it," she responded excitedly.

Victor's Café, located on 52nd Street, opened its doors in 1963 and is another hot spot for Cuban cooking and live music giving it a true Havana aura. Felipe and Marisol arrived, and since they had made an early reservation before they left the apartment, they were seated immediately.

"I think I'm going to have the Atlantic salmon," Marisol said.

"Me too. It looks good."

The server came over and took their order and came back promptly with their drinks.

"Materba para la señora." He poured Marisol her soda in a champagne glass. "Y para el caballero, Jupiña," and proceeded to do the same for Felipe. "Your appetizers will be coming out soon."

"Is this what you were whispering about to the waiter?" she asked, pointing at the glasses.

Felipe raised his glass. "Yes. Here's to us, our baby, and the adventure that's going to be our lives."

She picked up her glass and joined him in the toast. "Has Alex said anything about Tuesday?" she asked.

"We have nothing to worry about. It's going to be okay," he said trying to convince himself as well.

"I know we are. But I can't believe it's already on Tuesday. It feels like it was just yesterday that we were talking about this."

"I know. When this is all over and behind us, we're going to look for your brother."

Her eyes became misty at hearing the determination in his voice. The band started playing Enrique Iglesias' song "Hero," which had become their staple song.

"Dance with me," he asked her as he held out his hand.

She followed him to the dance floor, and although others had also joined them, the world existed at that moment only for them. By the time they returned to the table, their dinner was being served.

Skipping on coffee and dessert, Felipe paid for the check and they left. They headed southeast on 52nd Street toward Broadway and made a right on 5th Avenue. Shultz's Peanuts characters were the central players in Macy's window display that year. Marisol was fascinated with the lights and the big ivory piano keys that Linus and Charlie Brown were playing. The colorful Christmas trees with the appearance of white snow mesmerized Marisol. She looked up at her husband and gave him a big hug.

They walked along 5th Avenue in the brisk November night and enjoyed the displays and the busy and electrifying ambiance that the city provided. They had walked a lot and he could see Marisol was starting to get tired. He hailed a cab, and they went home.

* * *

"So what does a wife give her doctor husband for Christmas?" she asked Felipe as they were entering the apartment. He hung the keys on the hook, and they headed for the living room. Sitting cozy on the couch, he took a deep breath.

"Well, Christmas for me came early this year. So I'm all set," he responded.

"How so?" she asked.

He took her hand. "You know, when we got married, we

had a plan. Your pathway to citizenship would become a little easier—"

"And you would get the property your grandmother left you," she stopped to think for a minute."You haven't talked about that," she said.

"That's not important to me. You are what's important to me. And my brother called it right away."

"What did he say?" she asked.

"When I told him that I would marry you, he asked me if I was in love with you. I told him I cared about you, but we had only known each other a little over a month." He sighed. "I was full of it. I may not have wanted to admit it because it was so soon, but I loved you back then. You ever just know something because you just know?"

"Yes," she nodded.

"The only other thing I have ever been sure of was becoming a doctor. Then there was that whole thing with Sandra, and I thought maybe my attraction to you was a rebound. Then of course I thought that maybe you didn't feel the same way about me. But that feeling of certainty, that feeling of knowing with conviction that I wanted to marry you could only come from one place. The Holy Spirit. Speaking clearly and purposefully."

"Fatima told me the same thing. She kept insisting that there was something between us even the first time the three of us went out to eat. And then, after that, I kept getting 'trust in the Lord—'"

"'And lean not on your own understanding', Proverbs 3:5," he chimed in. "Me too, that's the scripture that was appearing everywhere for me. So it's clear that this was God's plan."

"I believe that. You said that you weren't sure how I felt about you when you asked me to marry you. I loved you when

I married you. But, like you, I wasn't sure how you felt. Then Fatima gave me that magazine and I tried their suggestions, but it just didn't feel natural. You know?"

He smiled at her." I remember. I love you exactly as you are."

"Well, Dr. Ortega, that works out perfectly because I love you too. When I first heard that a doctor had moved in next door, the first thing that I thought of was what in the world is a doctor doing here? And that was because I thought you were going to be stuck up. But then I looked in those dark brown eyes and that jet black hair and what I saw was a dedicated man with a heart of gold. I thought for sure once you knew my situation that you would run for the hills. But you didn't."

"No. You're stuck with me forever."

"Thank you, God."

He leaned over and kissed her. "Let's go to bed. It's been a long day and you need to rest."

"Let's do it."

Chapter 20

S unday came quicker than the Ortegas had anticipated. Marisol had rested all day Saturday while Felipe was called in to cover a shift for another doctor. She was fast asleep when he got home, and he didn't waste any time getting to bed because he was determined not to miss church on Sunday. He had not missed one service since he had started attending. Marisol snored softly next to him and it wasn't long before he was lost in his own slumber.

The Gonzalezes and the Ortegas had made it a tradition to walk to church together and Alex had become part of the group. Although it was cold, the sun was shining and there wasn't a cloud in the sky. Church members entered the sanctuary and were greeting one another as Pastor Melvin made his way to the front stopping along the way to chat.

"Alex, I'm glad to see you've been coming every week. The family keeps growing" Pastor Melvin warmly teased as he spotted them on his way to the pulpit.

"In more ways than you know Pastor," Felipe said.

"Oh?" he smiled as he inquired.

"We're having a baby," Marisol proudly said.

"Congratulations!" He hugged her and then approached Felipe for a handshake and a hug. As he embraced him, he whispered "We know that the immigration interview is Tuesday. We will be praying for a favorable outcome and peace to wash over you both and your families."

"Thank you, Pastor," Felipe responded.

The worship team led in a beautiful set, morning announcements were made, and the service began.

"Good Morning brothers and sisters" Pastor Melvin kindly addressed the church. "I hope everyone had a wonderful Thanksgiving and that you didn't eat too much like I did" he joked. Giggles filled the air as most could relate. "And now" he continued"the Christmas season is upon us. Let the shopping stress begin" he quipped, with the congregation nodding in agreement. "People worry about what gifts to buy, and whether their gifts will be appreciated or not. Others worry about spending money. Worry is our worst enemy. And that's what I would like to address today."

"When you worry, you have a divided mind" he continued "Worrying creates a culture of mistrust in your mind which leads to not trusting God. What does trusting God look like? Lean on him. Psalm 139 verses 1-6 tells us that he knows all things. He knows when we sit, and when we rise. He knows all of our thoughts. Before we say one word, he knows what we're going to say. He walks behind us and before us and has his mighty hand on us. And trusting him begins with having a relationship with him."

A pin dropping could not be heard as the Spirit of God moved and people were touched. Felipe and Marisol were transfixed knowing that Tuesday was a true test of faith for them. Each of them took brief notes in their Bibles, knowing they would have much to talk about when they got home.

"So, to wrap up, I want to leave you with some scriptures to keep in mind when you feel worry creeping up on you. Psalm 23:4 'Even when I walk through the darkest valley, I will not be afraid, for you are close beside me. Your rod and your staff will protect and comfort me'." No matter what you are facing today, cast out worry and remember that his grace is enough in every season.

Proverbs 3:5 reminds us to 'trust in the Lord with all your heart; do not depend on your own understanding. Seek his will in all you do, and he will show you which path to take.' Remember, when Jesus was crucified, his last words on the cross were 'It is finished' which means, the battle is over. Worry has no place in your life. Have a wonderfully blessed day. And all of God's people shouted—"

"Amen!" the congregation said in a chorus.

"Lunch on me!" Felipe announced to the group once they were outside.

* * *

They walked briskly to La Nueva España commenting on the service and deciding what they were going to eat. They made their way to their favorite table. Rosa, Fatima, and Marisol on one side with Bernie, Alex, and Felipe on the other, each facing their significant other.

"Tres Materbas, dos Jupiñas y un batido de Trigo" Felipe instructed the server on everyone's choice of beverage to expedite things.

"Marisol, you've taken a break from making wine," Fatima said as she buttered a piece of bread.

"I have because in January I am going to be really busy with school and other things" she smiled at Felipe.

"It's a hobby," Rosa added as she grabbed a mariquita. Plantain chips were her weakness.

"Oh, it is" Marisol agreed "I enjoyed doing it, but I never wanted to turn that into a career or anything like that."

"How was the hospital last night?" Bernie asked Felipe.

"Busy" Felipe responded as the server was putting down their drinks. They placed their order and Felipe resumed. "Two C-sections and three natural deliveries. I left around 2:00 a.m."

"The three of you have a long day on Tuesday," said Rosa addressing Felipe, Marisol, and Alex.

"The four of us" Fatima corrected her mom "I'm going too."

"Oh, then if you're going Bernie and I should go too," Rosa added looking at Alex for approval.

"The more family the better" Alex responded, "their appointment is at 10:00, but we need to get there earlier."

They continued to chat about the weather, news events, and the happenings in the building. A few minutes later their food arrived.

"Okay, I'm saying grace today" Alex smiled, demonstrating how much he resembled his brother's dimples. They all bowed their heads.

"Heavenly Father, we are grateful for the word that was given to us in church today. We also thank you for the food we are about to eat. In Jesus' name…"

The entire group said "Amen" in unison and dug into their food. The table was buzzing with the business of people eating.

Salt and pepper shakers, breadbasket, and silverware clanking mixed in with conversation. Marisol had ordered breaded steak with white rice and plantains. She took a small plate she had asked the waiter for and quietly poured some ketchup on it. She picked up the sugar dispenser and with the precision of a scientist studying a slide under the microscope proceeded to add a sprinkle to the ketchup.

Alex and Fatima were watching her. Fatima caught her mother's attention and pointed with her eyes at Marisol. Felipe caught sight of the silent communication and looked at his wife's plate. With his chin resting on his hand, he watched Marisol as she cut her steak into pieces. She was just about to dip a chunk into her concoction when she could feel their eyes fixated on her.

"Did you just add sugar to the ketchup?" Rosa inquired as she furrowed her eyebrows.

"I sure did" she confidently responded "sweet and sour. I should start experimenting with different sauces" she pondered as she savored her mix.

Raising his eyebrows, Bernie looked at Felipe.

"And we're only starting. These changes in taste buds get stronger as the pregnancy moves along" Felipe added.

"You mean cravings?" Fatima asked.

"I was avoiding having to use that word, but yes."

Everyone laughed except Marisol. "That's right. You laugh. Watch me create an incredible sauce. Watch," she said with a smile.

"Okay, you're all being unfair" Alex interceded with a half-smile.

"Thank you, Alex," Marisol said, grateful for her brother-in-law.

"Remember, this baby is part Italian, so the tomato sauce had to get in there somehow."

The laughter continued as Marisol responded, "I'm going to tell your mom you said that."

"When a daughter-in-law conspires with her mother-in-law, lookout," Rosa teased.

"Oh, I'm not done. Then there's the Hispanic side," Alex said.

"I got this one bro," Felipe said, "If it's a boy, we get him a white Guayabera and if it's a girl, we get her a Flamenco dress."

Everyone laughed at how cute an infant would look sporting these garments.

"You have to register for baby gifts. We have to organize a shower for you" Fatima added making a mental to-do list of her own.

"There's plenty of time. Do you have any baby names in mind?" Rosa asked.

"We're still talking about it. Did I ever tell you how I got my name?" Marisol asked.

They simultaneously nodded no.

"My mom wanted to name me Girasol"

"Oh, Sunflower. That's pretty. Why didn't she?" Fatima inquired.

"My dad said he didn't want people to see me like a seed. He wanted to name me Maria, after his mother. So, they compromised. Mari for Maria and Sol for Girasol."

"That was creative," Alex said.

She nodded and took a sip of her milkshake.

"How did you and Felipe get your names?" Fatima asked.

"My mother named me after my dad of course and he was named after Felipe the VI who was some prince," Felipe said as he rolled his eyes. "My brother was named after Alexander the Great," he added since Alex was chewing his food.

"That's right," Alex said as he drank some water. "My mom had this thing with kings and princes. Fatima how did you get your name?"

"It was my mom's sister's name. No queens or princesses here," she said.

"She is my older sister, and I am close to her. She is still devasted by her son's death. My nephew Armando was an FBI agent. He was killed in the line of duty, and he had just gotten married. Happened about three years ago."

"That's terrible," Marisol said.

"Where did they live?"

"They all lived in Rhode Island, but my nephew and his wife moved to Connecticut after they got married. He was transferred to work on a big human trafficking case. He didn't talk about his job at all. My sister told me once that agents were asked to take a polygraph every six months to ensure they were not talking about their cases."

"What part of Connecticut?" Felipe asked.

"I'm not sure."

"What does his wife do?" Alex asked.

"She's some kind of freelance writer. Her name is Araceli. I only saw her at their wedding and then the funeral. I felt so bad for her. To be a widow at such a young age."

"So, what do the two of you want to have first? A boy or a girl?" Rosa asked in an effort to change the tone of the conversation.

"As long as he or she is healthy, makes no difference to me" Marisol responded.

"Same here" Felipe agreed.

They ordered dessert and by the time they were completely

done, they had spent two hours as a family laughing and just enjoying each other's company. Felipe paid the bill and they walked home. They agreed to meet outside the building Tuesday at 8:30.

* * *

Felipe was watching Sunday night football in the living room and making sure they had all the paperwork they needed for Tuesday. He was going to the bathroom when he noticed Marisol standing in front of the full-length mirror. She was in her bra and panties and was standing sideways to see if she could catch the slightest glimpse of a pouch.

"You won't see anything for a while," he said.

"I know. I was about to take a shower and was just imagining what it will look like" she smiled.

He stood behind her and hugged her. They admired their reflection in the mirror.

"Call Julia tomorrow and set up an appointment" he suggested.

"Yep, it's on my list" she spun around "Okay, I'm getting cold, and I need to take a shower. She stood on her tippy toes and kissed him. He followed her in, and she noticed he was watching her undress.

"Didn't you have to go to the bathroom?" she teased.

"Yeah, but I got distracted by a beautiful woman."

"Where is she?" she playfully asked as she slid the shower curtain off to the side.

He walked over to the tub, stripped, and got in with her."She's standing right here," he whispered as he kissed her under the warm deluge of water emanating from the shower.

Chapter 21

The Ted Weiss Federal Building is located on Broadway and was a 45-minute trip from where the Ortega's and Gonzalezes lived. They got off at Chambers Street Station, where it was a five-minute walk to their destination. They stood in front of the giant 34 story building which appeared like it was Goliath ready to annihilate David. But, taking the example of David, who trusted God in the most abysmal circumstances, the group entered the building with confidence.

"Good Morning," Alex said to the receptionist, handing her his card, "I'm representing Marisol Ortega. Her interview is scheduled for 10:00 a.m." The group had seated themselves in the lobby while Alex checked in.

"Yes," the receptionist responded "the officer that will be conducting the interview is running a few minutes behind, but it shouldn't be much longer than your 10:00 a.m. appointment. A clerk will come by and give you instructions."

"Okay, thank you," Alex politely responded as he joined the

others and gave them an update.

"When we're done, where do you want to go for lunch?" Felipe asked Marisol.

"And this time it's on me" chimed in Bernie who had gently leaned his head back and closed his eyes to rest them."

"Where should we go?" Marisol asked Fatima and Rosa.

"Victor's Café," Fatima offered. The others gave nods of approval.

Rosa began to read, while Fatima played games on her phone. Forty minutes had gone by when a slender tall woman approached the group.

"Felipe and Marisol Ortega?" she asked.

"Right here," Felipe responded.

"Okay, your attorney can come in with you, the rest of you have to stay here. The officer will interview you both together and then separately." Fatima hugged Alex and Rosa and Bernie pulled Felipe and Marisol into a warm, comfortable embrace.

"Que Dios los acompañe," Rosa said, asking for God to go with them.

The three followed the clerk into a room with a conference table. Felipe, Marisol, and Alex sat on one side. The clerk left and the three had a few moments alone. *This is it* Marisol thought to herself. The loud beating of her heart was ringing in her ears. But, as soon as she called out *Heavenly Father*, she suddenly began to feel light and her heartbeat suddenly slowed down, *watch, and go before us. Give us the words to respond to the questions. When Felipe and I are separated for our interviews, we will not separate from you. Guide us with your wisdom and may your will be done.* Marisol was drawn back in when Alex started speaking.

"You will both be answering all the questions. My purpose

here is to look over the paperwork and as I've said before make sure the questions are not too out of hand. And, of course, to support you," he reassured Felipe and Marisol as they both smiled in agreement.

"Good Morning," Andre Brown, a tall African American distinguished-looking man said as he walked in.

"Good Morning," they responded as they stood, and each shook his hand

"I'm Mr. Brown, the USCIS officer who will be conducting your interview today," he proceeded to swear them in and then adjusted himself in the chair opposite them. "Okay, first I'm going to ask you for ID" he looked up and smiled.

Marisol gave her passport and tourist visa over to Mr. Brown who inspected each document carefully. Felipe provided his hospital ID, along with his state ID.

"Ahhh New York-Presbyterian Hospital. "My niece was born there," the officer reminisced. He looked at the file and knitted his brows a bit. "Counselor, your last name is Ortega as well. Any relation?"

"Felipe is my brother sir," Alex responded.

"Ahh," the officer said in understanding, "Okay, let's begin."

"Mrs. Ortega, where were you born?"

"Tegucigalpa, Honduras"

"And you Mr. Ortega?"

"Trumbull, Connecticut"

Mr. Brown asked to see their lease agreement, and one utility bill, on which Felipe had made sure they were both listed. He also provided a copy of their marriage license.

"Okay, and I have a copy of your I-30 petition and adjustment of status application. Have there been any changes since you filled out this paperwork?" He looked at both of them.

"My wife is about 6 weeks pregnant sir. I brought a copy of her lab results."

"I see," he nodded, becoming a little more serious.

Marisol felt Felipe squeeze her hand in a comforting way.

"You've been married two months and already expecting a baby, huh." Mr. Brown looked up from the paperwork and continued. "Well, why not" he smiled. "Mrs. Ortega let's start with you. How did you meet your husband?"

Marisol proceeded to inform him of how they met and how their relationship had progressed. The court officer couldn't help but notice how animated and enthusiastic Marisol recounted the memory. He darted his eyes toward Felipe who was looking at his wife and smiling and nodding his head as he was reminded of their history.

"Sounds like it was an adventure. Okay, Mr. Ortega, why don't you tell me about your first date."

"Well, it was more of a group date after church. We went to La Nueva España, up where we live."

"You had the churrasco," Marisol interrupted.

"I did," he confirmed, "It was good even though it was a little too well done for my taste."

"But you ate it," Marisol pointed and laughed.

Remembering where Felipe was, he cleared his throat and continued and made sure to not leave out Marisol's insistence on having her spaghetti sauce separate from her pasta. "And that was pretty much our first outing together."

"Okay. Let's move on. Mrs. Ortega, what kind of car does your husband drive?"

Marisol felt her heart sink.

* * *

"What's taking so long?" Fatima impatiently questioned as she paced.

"Pacing back and forth like that is not going to help at all" Rosa said to her daughter.

The elevator opened and out came Bernie with a tray that held coffee, followed by Victoria and Felipe Senior. "Look who I ran into."

"We tried to get here on time, but the traffic was awful on the George Washington Bridge. Any news?" Felipe Senior inquired.

"No. They've been in there for about fifteen minutes" Fatima reported dismayed.

"Don't worry honey" Victoria said, "it's going to work out. You'll see."

"I'm glad you both made it before they come out. It's going to mean the world to Felipe and of course Marisol. Bernie and I are treating everyone to lunch after" Rosa said to them.

"That sounds good. How is Marisol feeling?" Victoria asked with a concerned tone.

"She's been okay the past few days. This morning she was a little queasy but was able to eat some breakfast" Rosa responded.

"That's good. At least she's not throwing up her dinner consistently."

"She's like a daughter to me and Bernie. She's a good girl" Rosa said, her voice shaking and eyes tearing.

Victoria put his arm around Rosa in solidarity.

* * *

"Mrs. Ortega" Mr. Brown repeated, "What kind of car does

your husband drive?"

"I've only seen it once, and I don't remember" she meekly responded.

"Sir, a few days after we met, I drove my car back to Connecticut and took the train back into the city," Felipe explained. Her knight in shining armor to the rescue.

"I see," he responded a little icy.

"Dr. Ortega, where does the superintendent of your building live?"

"He lives in an apartment in the basement, not far from the trash chute. His name is Hector, and he can't be bothered on Wednesdays because he has his kids after school. "

"Okay, Mrs. Ortega, when did you and your husband move it together?"

Marisol's meekness turned into indignation. "After we were married, sir" she responded crossly.

Felipe suppressed his smile.

"I won't ask if you have been intimate because that's obvious," quipped Mr. Brown. Realizing that he had tripped a sensitive nerve, he moved on with other questions that they swiftly responded to individually and sometimes together.

"Mrs. Ortega, you need to come with me."

Marisol froze for a second and then felt a complete peace wash over her. Felipe stood up with her and gave her a kiss.

"I'll see you soon," he whispered.

She picked up her purse and followed Mr. Brown. He escorted her to another room where there was another USCIS officer.

* * *

"Make yourself comfortable, Mrs. Ortega. Ms. Miller, can I see you outside for a moment?" Mr. Brown inquired.

Mr. Brown spoke with Ms. Miller for what seemed like an eternity before she came back inside. She settled herself and opened the file.

"Okay, Marisol. May I call you Marisol?" the middle-aged woman asked.

"Yes, of course."

"Okay, I'm going to ask you a couple of questions. Tell me when your relationship with Mr. Ortega turned romantic."

For a few seconds, Marisol played a montage of her relationship with Felipe in her mind. Their first meeting on the fire escape. The day they made wine. The black bean episode and who could ever forget the whipped cream caper. Before she knew it, she was smiling because she knew exactly what she had to say.

* * *

Mr. Brown settled himself back in the other conference room with Felipe and Alex.

"Okay, Mr. Ortega. I have some questions I will be asking you as well. Tell me at what point did your relationship with Mrs. Ortega become romantic?" Mr. Brown asked as he looked up.

Felipe smiled before he responded, "There was something about her the first time we met on that fire escape, but I didn't see it then. And, not long after that, we made wine in her apartment and I would have to say that's when I really started to see her differently. By the time we had our cookoff one Saturday where due to a blender malfunction we ended up covered in black beans, I was totally in love with her. I love her company. When I leave work, I can't wait to get home and watch television with her. She's the first person I want to talk to about my day. She's my best friend."

* * *

"So, you see," Marisol added to the response she had given Ms. Miller, mirroring Felipe's account "the time we made wine in my apartment, I was already seeing him differently."

"Okay," Ms. Miller responded as she feverishly took notes.

* * *

"We attend church every Sunday," Felipe responded to Mr. Brown, "even when we were just friends."

* * *

"I still remember the first time we went to church," Marisol informed Ms. Miller. "We were just friends then and once he started coming with me, he was hooked." Marisol smiled at the memory.

* * *

"Okay," Ms. Miller stated, "one more question. What is your song together?"

"Hero by Enrique Iglesias," Marisol responded as her eyes filled with tears.

* * *

"Mr. Ortega, every couple has a song that they claim as theirs. What's yours?

"Hero by Enrique Iglesias" Felipe responded.

As Mr. Brown was writing, the door opened, and Ms. Miller was escorting Marisol back.

"Mr. Brown, a minute?"

"Yes, I was just about to go see if you ladies were all set."

He stepped outside to conference with Ms. Miller. Marisol sat down and smiled at Felipe who took her hand in his.

"Okay, the interview is pretty much done. Is there anything either one of you would like to add?" Mr. Brown proposed as he took his seat.

"I would," Felipe stated as he nodded his head. "Marisol can't go to sleep unless all the closet doors in the apartment are shut. She sleeps with her hair in a bun, and she has watched every episode of *Friends* at least a dozen times. Except for the one, of course where Ross and Rachel break up because you see, it's sad. She's taken a break from it, but when we met, she made her own wine. And it is spectacular. Most nights I work, she waits up for me. We have a snack together and then watch TV or go to bed. We attend church every Sunday and then go out to eat with our friends. The reason why I'm saying all this is because we've answered a lot of questions today. But I wanted you to know some of the important things I know about my wife." He managed to overpower the pool of tears that had formed in his eyes and hugged Marisol closely to him.

Mr. Brown had listened intently, his expression softening a little. "Mrs. Ortega, is there anything you would like to add?"

"Yes, there is," she responded as she brushed the tears away from her face. "Felipe somehow ends up walking around the apartment with only one sock on. He has a cup of American coffee first thing in the morning and follows up with a cup of Café con Leche. He talks to whatever shows he's watching as if he's directing them. Sometimes two at a time. He is patient, kind and compassionate, and extremely romantic. He doesn't need a holiday or occasion to bring me flowers. Our lives are simple, but we cherish every day."

Mr. Brown's face had completely softened up. He put his pen down and casually took off his glasses placing them on the table as well.

"Let me ask you both something" he started in a casual, friendly tone "And either one of you can answer" he paused again carefully choosing his words, "tell me about your first fight."

Marisol and Felipe looked at each other and snickered. As if she was in school, Marisol raised her hand and said, "I've got this."

Felipe smiled and said, "Go for it."

"I will" she sassed back playfully. "So," she turned her attention to Mr. Brown. "Felipe came home one night, and I was watching an episode of *Friends* where this couple, Ross and Rachel, fought and he cheated on her."

"No, no, no," Felipe interrupted with a smile as he was shaking his head no "Be fair and tell the whole story," he said to Marisol with a half-smile. Turning his attention to Mr. Brown, he continued, "Rachel told Ross she wanted a break. So, when he slept with the other girl, as far as he knew they were broken up."

Marisol was shaking her head, "broken up smocken up," she mocked. "He should have known better and if he really loved her, he would have not done what he did, right?"She redirected herself to Mr. Brown and Alex, who busied himself right away with paperwork.

"I'm staying out of this. I'm just a relative" Alex joked. Mr. Brown laughed at the family dynamics.

"Okay, I've heard what I need to hear, and I am ready to make a decision."

Felipe took Marisol's hand as they both grew serious again.

"The questions that we ask when we conduct these interviews are standard, and it's hard to pick ones that will suit each couple. We listen to the answers, but we also watch body language. When people answer the questions too perfectly, that raises a flag. So, Mrs. Ortega, when you said that you did not know the type of car your husband has and then he offered the explanation, it was an honest answer and one that made sense. It's impossible to get every detail correct. I've been married for over 40 years, and there are still things about my wife and kids that would probably be news to me. But I will tell you what you can't fake. And that's the way that you Mr. Ortega look at your wife when she's talking and how you Mrs. Ortega look at your husband when he's speaking. When you each spoke at the end, the sincerity in your voices would have been impossible to forge. When I met with Mrs. Miller to compare answers, it's as if you had been in each other's heads. You spoke from the heart and you can't fake that."

The silence in the room was thickening and Marisol's stomach started to growl loudly.

"We're almost done here. We need to get that baby fed" he joked as the others chuckled.

"What was a flag, in this case, was the short amount of time you have been married and the fact that you are already expecting a baby."

Marisol felt her heartbeat increase and Felipe could hear her breathing become shallow.

"However," Mr. Brown continued, "Anyone with eyes can see that you are two wonderful people who didn't waste any time in falling in love. I am satisfied that your marriage is as authentic and real as it could possibly be" he paused and looked over at Alex who had been fidgeting with a rubber band. "Counselor," he said as a way to get his attention. "You're up. Are you ready to process some forms?

"Yes sir" Alex smiled.

He watched Mr. Brown pick up the stamp and mark Marisol's application as "temporary evidence of lawful admission." Marisol was on her way to citizenship. Felipe and Marisol hugged as Mr. Brown looked on and smiled. Once they were finished with all the paperwork, he shook hands with them both and wished them the best of luck. Once he had left the room, Felipe walked over to his brother. They looked at each other and then hugged a tight bear hug each of them with tears blinding their eyes.

"Thank you, bro," Felipe whispered in his brother's ear.

"I didn't do anything. You guys were ready," he responded.

"We were ready because you guided us," Felipe responded.

Both brothers suddenly looked down at Marisol who was still sitting down and sobbing aloud.

"Babe, what's wrong? It's over" Felipe reassured her.

"I know" she sobbed even more.

"Why are you crying then?"

"Because" she took several breaths, "because I'm so hap-pyyyyy" she managed to say between sobs."

"Okay, it's okay" Felipe reassured her as he held her. "Come on. Let's get out of here."

Alex picked up all their paperwork and folders and followed
them out.

* * *

"Oh my God, here they come, and Marisol is crying. Ay Dios
mio." Fatima announced to the group as they saw them coming
through the double doors. After Felipe Senior and Victoria
had arrived, more reinforcements from the church had shown
up. Their temporary fears were allayed when they saw Alex
in the back with a raised arm, giving them the thumbs up.

Bernie and Rosa hugged as did Felipe Senior and Victoria,
which was all that Felipe, Marisol, and Alex were able to see
until they got closer. Pastor Melvin was hugging Mathew,
one of the elders of the church. Yolanda and Maribel, two
congregants that had been praying over the situation, were
also present. There was victory in the air.

Felipe had managed to calm Marisol down until she saw the
crowd of people that had come to support her, and she started
blubbering again. Felipe didn't even say a word. He just stood
there and held his wife until she was calm again.

"Gente," Felipe Senior attempted to be the voice of reason,
"People," he repeated in case they didn't hear him the first time,
"let's move outside and continue the celebration there."

Bernie and Pastor Melvin took his cue and started shepherd-
ing everyone outside.

Victoria was hugging Marisol and Felipe when Bernie made
an announcement.

"Let's all head to Victor's Café. Rosa called a couple of hours
ago and made reservations. And I'm telling everyone right

now that it's on me. And I don't want to hear another word. Eh dicho, caso cerrado!" Everyone laughed at his reference to the show. Five cabs were hailed and before they knew it, they were seated at their table engaging in lively conversations.

Chapter 22

J uly 2016

The rest of Marisol's pregnancy was smooth, and she was able to complete a semester online with Liberty University, earning straight As. She had continued working part-time at La Esquinita but stopped in June so she could prepare for the baby's arrival.

Felipe was still working at the hospital and was going to take paternity leave as soon as Marisol had the baby. Alex and Fatima were still going strong, and Felipe had hinted to Marisol that a proposal would be imminent. Bernie and Rosa were eagerly waiting to become surrogate grandparents to the baby and were already creating a schedule with Felipe Senior and Victoria for babysitting and visits.

It was Tuesday, July 5th, and not wanting to wake Felipe, Marisol was rummaging through the closet in the dark looking for a pair of shoes to wear. She had bought the same style of shoes in different colors because they were the only ones that didn't hurt swelling feet. After putting on her shoes in the dark, she straightened out the lilac maternity dress that Victoria had sent her for Mother's Day from the baby. She kissed a snoring Felipe goodbye and headed out.

She had several errands to run and had to meet him at the doctor's office for her weekly appointment. The post office, cleaners, and bank were on the list and she began to notice that no matter where she went, people were staring at her feet and snickering. Her stomach being so big, she was not able to see her feet. She thought about stopping to see Fatima at work, but she was running late for her appointment and she knew Felipe had to go to work right after.

"Hey honey," she said to Felipe as he walked into the doctor's office already dressed in scrubs and ready for work. He kissed her hello and sat beside her.

"Were you able to do everything you wanted to do? You know, I could have taken some of the errands for you."

"I was fine, but my feet must be really swollen," she said. He looked at her feet and his eyes widened as he saw the atrocity. "All day long, people kept staring at my feet," she informed him.

"Babe, that's because you're wearing two different colored shoes," he told her, trying desperately to masquerade a grin.

"No way!" she exclaimed. He got a kick out of watching her attempt to look at her feet. She first tried to lean over and almost toppled on top of him. Then, she tried getting a side angle. No avail. Out of breath, she finally sat down. He leaned over and took both shoes off to show her." He laughed and then kissed her cheek.

"Mrs. Ortega, you can come in" Lisa, the doctor's assistant said as she held the door open. Marisol leaned back to gain momentum so she could get up and then Felipe gently took her arm and helped her.

"Half a pound. That's not too bad. You've done really well with your weight" Lisa complimented Marisol. "Okay, Dr. Torres will be here shortly."

She left them in the room and Felipe was looking at the doctor's bulletin board which was covered with pictures of babies she had delivered. He smiled knowing that it could be any day now that their baby would be featured as well.

"Hello!" Dr. Torres greeted her colleague and his wife with a hug for each. "How are we feeling today?"

"Big," Marisol stated as she laughed. The doctor took her blood pressure, and then checked for dilation."

"Okay, nothing yet, but your due date is Friday, which means that it could be any time either two weeks early or two weeks late, but I'm sure Felipe has you well trained" she laughed and so did he. "I know that you have met with Dr. Menendez, and you know that who delivers your baby will depend on who's on call," she clarified to a disgruntled Marisol. She said goodbye and left Felipe to help Marisol dress again.

"I know you want Dr. Torres to deliver the baby, but it could be Tomas," Felipe looked at Marisol as he was putting her mismatched shoes on, "why are you rolling your eyes. He's a great doctor and a nice guy."

"I know he is. But he's young and he's a guy and you know I feel funny about stuff like that," she whined.

"I just want you to be prepared in case it's not Julia."

"I guess," she conceded.

"Fatima is meeting me here, so she can walk you back," Felipe instructed Marisol.

"Is that really necessary?" she asked.

"Yes, it is. She's staying with you until I get home tonight, and I think Rosa and Bernie are coming over too."

"I'm not helpless you know," she said.

"I never said you were. But, what if your water breaks? Or you start having labor pains. Do it for me. I will work better knowing that you're not alone."

"Okay," she said as she gave in.

* * *

It was the schedule they would keep for the next two weeks. The Gonzalez clan and Alex would keep her company until Felipe got home from work. Marisol's complaints fell on deaf ears until she gave up and just allowed herself to be pampered.

On July 23rd, they had just eaten dinner and had sat down to watch *Caso Cerrado*. Alex had just gotten home from work, showered, and headed over to Felipe's where the group had gathered to keep Marisol company. He was eating his dinner in the kitchen while Fatima kept him company.

"Fatima!" they heard Rosa calling out "Marisol's water broke. Alex, call your brother and tell him we're on our way."

"Rosa it could be hours before I go into labor," Marisol protested as she turned on the shower.

"Niña! This is no time to take a shower. What if you start having pains or you fall?"

"I'll be careful," she promised.

Once she was out of the shower, she blow-dried her hair and then started putting makeup on.

"Oye," Fatima called out to her as she entered the bathroom "Where exactly do you think you're going? You're not posing for Vogue. You're having a baby!"

"I know" Marisol nonchalantly responded. "And if I'm going

to be in pain," she said as she sprayed herself with cologne, "I might as well look good." As she finished her sentence, she felt a sharp pain pierce her back so badly that she almost fell where she was standing. She breathed in and out. In and out. "See?" she pointed out to Fatima, "Piece of cake."

"Marisol Colucci Ortega if you don't get out here right now," Rosa frantically stated.

"Here I am. I have to call Felipe" she said.

"No, I called him, and he's already called me twice to see why we're not there yet."

"Taxis are here," Bernie announced.

* * *

Felipe was already in the receiving area when they arrived. "Why did it take so long?" he asked.

"La señora insisted on taking a shower and getting ready like she was la Reina de Washington Heights," Fatima tattled on Marisol.

"Never mind me thinking I'm the queen of Washington Heights.I didn't want to look like a rag doll."

"Have you had contractions?" Felipe inquired in full doctor mode.

"Just one really big one," she whispered.

"Okay," he took a deep breath and just blurted out what he was dreading to tell her. "Dr. Torres is not on call. It's Tomas Menendez "

She opened her mouth to speak and before she could utter a syllable, he asked her, "Do you trust me?"

"Of course, I trust you," she responded softly.

"Okay, it's going to be fine.

"I guess," she acquiesced.

"That's my girl." He kissed her and proceeded to wheel her to her room.

"Dr. Ortega, you're on the other side tonight" the nurse greeted her colleague.

"Yes, different perspective tonight," he pleasantly responded.

The nurse gave Marisol a gown and helped her to the bathroom to change.

"Okay, you've dilated two centimeters. When was your last contraction?"

"I had one at 6:00 and then another one at 7:30."

Felipe exchanged glances with the nurse because he knew what the recommendation was going to be if Marisol's contractions didn't become more consistent.

"Okay, I'm going to hook up this monitor to your belly and it will monitor your contractions. Remember to do your breathing and dad you keep track of the times she has them. The doctor is going to come in to insert a fetal heart monitor. This helps us keep tabs on the baby's heartbeat. Okay? Will you be having an epidural?"

"No, I hate needles," Marisol innocently replied.

The nurse smiled and gave them their privacy.

Felipe arranged the pillow a certain way so that she would be more comfortable. She sighed heavily and looked at Felipe. "Look at you," she said. "From doctor to daddy."

"No, look at you" he responded.

"You look absolutely beautiful. Why don't you close your eyes for a little while?"

"Okay," she responded.

* * *

An hour had gone by and Marisol had not had another contraction. She was at three centimeters. She stirred when she heard Felipe talking to her doctor. They were conversing like old friends.

"Hi Dr. Menendez"

"Hola Marisol. Please, call me Tomas. I'm going to check you again" he said as he gently pulled the covers over. He could feel her tightening her legs.

"Just relax. The more you relax, the less pressure you will feel."

"Babe, take a deep breath and let it out slowly" Felipe instructed her. She obliged and realized that the breathing was helping.

"Okay," the doctor announced as he took off the gloves. "You are at 4 centimeters, which is good, but your contractions are not consistent. We're going to have to induce labor."

"And how are we going to do that?" Marisol inquired.

"We're going to give you Pitocin. It's going to make the contractions stronger, but it will speed up the labor." He gave instructions to the nurse and left.

Marisol's eyes began to fill with tears. "Why are you crying?" Felipe asked her.

"I'm just afraid that something might go wrong," she said quietly

"Nothing is going wrong" he assured her, "I've had to do this for patients. I've never lied to you, so I'm going to tell you that the contractions will be strong. So, get some rest now."

"How long does it take for that stuff to take effect," she asked as the nurse was putting it into her IV."

"A couple of hours," the nurse responded.

Marisol looked at Felipe who nodded in agreement. "It takes

about two hours. I'm going to step out to the lobby and update the crew. Okay?"

"Okay. Come right back!"

"I promise" he kissed her and stepped out.

* * *

Fatima and Rosa ran toward Felipe as they saw him coming out.

"What's going on?" Fatima eagerly asked as the rest of the family gathered around Felipe.

"They have to induce labor because her contractions are inconsistent even though she is dilating."

"Oh boy," Bernie slipped.

"Is that bad?" Fatima asked.

"No, it's just that she's going to have very strong contractions," Rosa said.

"And she didn't want an epidural because she hates needles," Fatima recalled.

"Where's my brother?" Felipe asked.

"He went to get us coffee. He also called your parents and they're on their way."

"Do you want to see her before she goes into the rough part of labor?" Felipe asked.

"No," Rosa responded, "let her rest."

* * *

Marisol was dozing in and out when Felipe came back into the room.

"How's everybody doing?" she asked with her eyes closed.

"Good. They send their love. They're staying, and my parents are on their way," he responded as he checked her IV and glanced at her chart.

"I thought you said you wouldn't do that," she smiled.

"I'm just checking to see what's going on," he responded. "Close your eyes and try to rest."

She closed her eyes for what felt like five minutes, but forty minutes had passed when she opened her eyes as if she had been hit with a bat.

Felipe had been resting his eyes sitting on a chair when he heard her.

"Felipe..." Marisol tried to sit up but found that the pain was so excruciating she couldn't move. "I think something's wrong."

"No. Nothing is wrong," Felipe responded immediately taking her hand. "The Pitocin is kicking in." It broke his heart to see her writhing in pain.

"Okay, Mrs. Ortega, let's see how we're coming along," the nurse said as she prepared to check on Marisol. "You are at 5 centimeters. The contractions are going to get stronger, and you are going to have the urge to push, but you can't. You have to breathe through them."

"Like you did when we took the Lamaze classes."

"How far apart are they?" the nurse asked Felipe as Marisol started to pant.

"She had one about two minutes ago and it looks like here comes another one."

"Ya think!" Marisol retorted as she attempted to start her breathing.

Felipe grabbed her hand. He did the breathing exercise with her and watched the little pearls of sweat that were forming on her forehead and upper lip.

"You did good babe. You're doing great," Felipe encouraged her as he fed her ice chips.

Two minutes had gone by and she was attacking another contraction.

"Okay, let me think," she panted as she came down from another contraction.

"Think about what hon?"

"I have an idea. We can do this tomorrow," She stated trying to get up as if she could go home and leave the pain right on the bed.

"No, no." He started to hold her down so she could not get up."It doesn't work that way," he gently said.

"I'll come back tomorrow. I pro…,"she didn't even get the word out before she was overtaken by another contraction. No time to gear up for it. No warning. Just a razor-sharp pain shooting across her back and tightening her stomach.

Watching his wife in pain was wearing on Felipe. As a professional courtesy, Felipe notified the doctor and asked if she could be given a sedative so she could relax between contractions. The nurse came in and administered a small dose into her IV.

It was 9:00 a.m. and Marisol had spent the entire night in active labor, not being able to push with wrenching contractions that left her weak. She had been able to rest for a minute or two between contractions.

During one of brief periods of respite, Marisol looked around the room. The sun was shining through the curtains, so she knew it was morning. Felipe was sitting in a chair right next to her bed fighting sleep. She turned her head and saw that Tomas was sitting on the bed.

Chapter 22

"How long have you been here?" she asked the doctor.

"All night," Felipe responded for him, as Tomas nodded his head.

Marisol's breathing began to labor as she struggled to deal with another revolting contraction that was ripping through her body.

"Okay, you've got this," Felipe encouraged her as he stood up and supported her.

"Remember your focal point," Dr. Menendez encouraged as he checked for dilation.

Felipe wiped her face gently with a washcloth as the contraction was coming down.

"Why are you smiling," Marisol asked Felipe.

"Because I'm thinking about the day we made wine."

She smiled at the memory.

He continued as a means to distract her. "Remember the day we both got covered in black beans? And, what about the time you bobbed for apples and dunked your head in the water?"

She laughed and it was a welcome distraction. Marisol had started her labor looking beautiful and with a glow that could light up any room. Twelve hours later, her torso resembled a pretzel. Tomas, who was sitting to her right on the bed, housed her right foot on his right thigh.

Her left leg was dangling from the side of the bed and her body had shifted so she was basically in a diagonal position. Felipe tried to use this respite to change her position.

"Let's straighten you out," Felipe gently said but he was too late. The laughing had stopped, and the torturous agony had commenced.

"Don't touch," she yelled, "I can stay like this, right Tomas?" She was in so much pain that modesty and timidity had long left her. And so had the last contraction, but not for long. Marisol had just started to come down a little when again the pain gripped her.

"Oh, there's a big one coming," Felipe announced as Marisol just stared at him panting.

"Come on babe, breeeeathe"

"Oh my God Felipe. Tell me one more time to breeeathe and I'm going to clock you over the head when I get out of this mess!"

"Okay, we're ready to go!" Tomas announced. Marisol was rushed into the delivery room with a team already standing by. Felipe was already in scrubs and standing to her right.

"Okay, Marisol, push," Tomas said.

Felipe and one of the nurses assisted her to a slightly raised position and she pushed with all her might turning bright red. A few cycles of this pattern and the doctor realized that the second she stopped pushing, the baby would descend further back.

Felipe had caught on with the problem that was occurring, and it was confirmed when he saw Tomas pulling out the vacuum.

"What are you going to do with that mini-toilet plunger?" Marisol asked during her thirty-second pause from pain.

"This goes on a portion of the baby's skull. When you push again, this will help the baby come out. You made the baby too comfortable and he or she is refusing to come out," Tomas said. "This is almost over, and you've done great," he added.

"Babe, I'm right here," Felipe told Marisol as he was switching places with one of the nurses. She had one nurse on each side of her.

"Felipe, on three as soon as the next one comes," Tomas

instructed.

As soon as Marisol pushed again. She pushed so hard that she popped blood vessels in her face. Simultaneously, Felipe leaned over his wife and with his arm kneaded her stomach to guide the baby out.

"It's a girl!" Tomas announced as he pulled the baby out.

Marisol was exhausted as tears started streaming down her face. Felipe cut the cord, and pictures were taken. He removed his mask and showered his wife with kisses.

"Abigail Grace," a depleted Marisol whispered to him before she closed her eyes

"Abigail Grace" he repeated.

* * *

"I'm giving birth at home," a frustrated Fatima announced. "It' been hours and we know nothing."

"Be patient. This takes a while," said Alex smiling at her proclamation

"Patience? Esta niña?" Bernie added.

Felipe Senior had just come back with round four of cafe con leche and Victoria and Rosa had been chatting when they saw Felipe with a smile coming through the double doors, almost fifteen hours after Marisol had gone into labor.

"We have a girl!" he announced excitedly. Hugs, kisses, and cheers were exchanged until the questions began.

"Bueno, give us the stats and how is Marisol!" Fatima asked on behalf of the group.

"Abigail Grace is 7 pounds 13 ounces and 21 ½ inches long," he responded as he pulled up pictures. "Marisol is just completely worn out. This was extremely taxing for her and right before I came out, she fainted, which is normal after a difficult labor."

Fatima was smiling and still scrutinizing the pictures trying to decide who Abigail resembled the most. "Oye, she has Marisol's ears, but I think she's going to have your dimples. Olvidate, she's definitely a chip off the old brick"

"Block" the entire group chorused, except Alex.

"I knew what she meant," Alex said, looking on with her at the pictures of his niece.

Felipe took them in small groups to see the baby and then the family headed back to the apartment for some rest. Felipe Sr. and Victoria went with Bernie and Rosa. Although Alex had offered, the ladies wanted to collaborate to create a help schedule for the following week. Alex and Fatima went to their respective apartments and the plan was for the group to go see Marisol later in the afternoon.

* * *

Marisol opened her eyes and saw her daughter in the portable rolling crib that babies are placed in. She was dressed in the lilac onesie Marisol had brought to the hospital.

"She's as beautiful as her mom," she heard Felipe say.

"I can't believe you're still here. You must be exhausted."

"I'm good. My brother brought me a change of clothes and I took a shower in the doctor's lounge and slept a couple of hours. The most important thing here is how are you feeling?"

"Okay."

"Liar," he said as he kissed her head.

"Actually, I want to go to the bathroom and not in that little pan," she said as she motioned to get up.

"Wait…" he said as he gently stilled her with his arm, "you have to do this slowly." He had her first sit up and then slowly assisted her in swinging her legs around the bed. "Lean on me completely." Taking small steps, he helped her get to the bathroom.

"Oh no," she gasped as she caught her reflection in the mirror. "Why does it look like I have a bird's nest on my head?" she inquired as she felt the knotted hair at the top of her head. "I don't remember my face being this fat when I got here," she said upon further inspection.

"You just had a baby, and your body has been through a lot."

"I guess," Marisol sighed as she brushed her teeth. "I want to take a shower."

"You have to let me help you," he said with authority.

"Yes, sir," she responded with a smile.

* * *

"Oye, you're all put together," Fatima said as she glanced at Alex to make sure she had said it right. He gave her a smile and a wink assuring her that it was fine. Truth be told, she could have said anything, and he would have found it to be poetic.

"I had some help," Marisol laughed as she looked at her husband.

"The baby is beautiful," Rosa gushed.

"She really is," proud Grandmother Victoria agreed.

Bernie and Felipe had brought some pastelitos and I con leche for everyone. It was a treat for Marisol to be indulged with her favorite snack.

"Hola, ¿cómo andamos por aquí?" Tomas inquired of the

group.

"Hey!" Felipe greeted his colleague and friend, "Come have some coffee. I bought two extras."

"I'm on my way out, but I wanted to stop in for a few minutes," he responded as he took Felipe up on his offer. "We changed Lourdes' birthday dinner for tonight."

"I still can't believe you canceled because of us."

"Canceled what?" a confused Marisol asked.

"Yesterday was his wife's birthday and they were all going out to dinner. He postponed his plans to stay with us."

"Are you serious? Marisol said.

"You were having a difficult time, and I wasn't going to have another doctor come in. And we doctors take care of each other," he said to Felipe.

"We certainly do."

"Marisol, you gave birth to that little girl naturally because it was you. You are one tough lady" Tomas said.

"Yes, she is," her beaming husband concurred.

"Bueno, me voy. I'll see you in the office in two weeks. I left the discharge papers ready, and you can go home in the morning," he said to Marisol as he leaned over and kissed her on the cheek. He shook hands with Felipe and the rest of the family and left.

The Gonzalezes and the Ortegas stayed for about another hour and eventually left. Rosa and Victoria had planned a homecoming and wanted to do some last-minute shopping before Marisol and the baby came home.

* * *

"You have to get some rest," Felipe told Marisol.

"You should go home," she replied.

"Nope. I'm not leaving my girls," he said gazing at Marisol and his daughter. I'm going to rest on the couch and if it gets too uncomfortable, I'll take a nap in the lounge."

"Are you sure?"

"I'm sure. And I'm even more sure that we should pray before you fall asleep. I'll lead."

"Okay," she replied sleepily.

"Heavenly Father, we thank you for this day. I thank you that Marisol gave birth without any complications. I thank you that Abigail Grace is healthy, and we ask for your loving grace and guidance as we bring her up to always honor you. You have never failed us, Lord. Even when things looked dark, like your word says, the light prevailed. We thank you for our family and for the life that waits ahead of us. Let it be filled with good memories and adventures. In Jesus' name…"

"Amen," they said in unison.

"I love you," Marisol whispered.

"Right back at you Ortega," he replied.

Chapter 23

Epilogue
May 2018

Felipe and Marisol were four months shy of their third wedding anniversary and Abigail Grace was three months shy of her second birthday. Marisol received her green card and works as a court reporter in downtown Manhattan. Bernie continues working with Felipe at New York-Presbyterian Hospital and Rosa retired from La Esquinita even though since she is the owner, she goes in once a week to do payroll and other paperwork. Felipe Senior and Victoria still live in Connecticut but commute often to see their family.

Upon graduating from John Jay College, Fatima joined the police academy and works for the NYPD. She married Alex a year after she joined the force.

The four of them were getting ready to take a relaxing getaway to the New England states. But what they never imagined was the web of danger for which they were headed and the warped surprises that would catch them unguarded.

* * *

About three hours away in Stonington Connecticut, Araceli Cancio was starting to close the jewelry kiosk in the mall where she worked. With Mother's Day approaching, it had been a busy night. But that had not stopped her from being able to gaze at the handsome man working at the shoe store directly in front of the kiosk. He was about 5'10 with dark brown hair and hazel eyes. She had never seen him dressed in anything, but a suit and he was always well-groomed.

They had both started working at their respective stores within weeks of each other and she had caught him at times looking at her. She often wondered if he had noticed her stealing glances every chance she had. But neither had dared to approach the other until tonight.

Araceli had put the cash and checks in the night deposit envelope, which she placed next to her purse. She had just locked up the cabinets below the counter when she realized that six men were surrounding the kiosk.

"Good night for sales. You look like you could use a little fun tonight," one asked.

"Yeah, and I bet with the money you have in that bag, we could have a good time."

They continued to taunt her until they heard a loud, rattling noise, which was the handsome shoe store salesman pulling up the gate to the store. He was carrying a bat and walked toward the kiosk with a purpose and attitude that could only draw respect.

247

"Ready to go babe?" he asked Araceli as he tossed the bat from one hand to another.

Picking up on his vibe, she followed along. "Yep. I was just closing up the cabinets," she responded to the handsome acquaintance.

"Okay, gentlemen is there something we can help you with? The store is closed, but I'm sure an accommodation can be made, with Mother's Day coming up and all." He spoke with determination and grit.

The group of men looked at each other, looked at him, and just walked away.

"That was close. Thank you so much," Araceli said.

"No worries. Get your stuff and I'll take you home. You can't take a bus every night with all that cash," he said as he turned on his heel and headed back to lock up.

Okay, now I know he's been looking at me. How does he know I take the bus? Araceli thought.

"Wait a second," Araceli protested. "I don't even know your name or anything about you."

He stopped and turned.

"My name is Anthony. Anthony Colucci."

About the Author

Maria Rivera lived in the Washington Heights area of New York City for eleven years. She obtained a BA in English with a minor in Criminal Justice and an MS in Teaching Secondary English. She taught middle school and high school English in Florida and currently lives in Connecticut with her husband where she continues to teach high school English. *Chasing The Wind* is her debut novel. *Chasing Shadows* coming in 2022.

Made in the USA
Las Vegas, NV
02 June 2021

24031919R10152